They named me GERTRUDE STEIN

By Ellen Wilson

American Painter in Paris: A Life of Mary Cassatt
They Named Me Gertrude Stein

They named me
GERTRUDE STEIN

Ellen Wilson

Farrar, Straus and Giroux/New York

To my editor, Clare Costello

ACKNOWLEDGMENTS

It is with very real pleasure that I acknowledge my debt to various scholars and friends who contributed much to my background in the writing of this book. It would be impossible to name them all, but among the many to whom I am warmly grateful are the following:

The staff of the Lilly Library of Indiana University, especially Mrs. James A. Work, who produced rare and limited editions of Gertrude Stein's books for my perusal; the director of the Lilly Library, David A. Randall, who gave me a letter of introduction to Donald C. Gallup at Yale, who, as curator, made it possible for me to work in the Gertrude Stein Collection of the Yale Collection of American Literature; and to Mrs. Anne Whelpley there, who let me examine manuscripts and hundreds of Stein photographs and showed me the chairs whose covers Alice Toklas had worked from Picasso designs, and some of the embroidered waistcoats that Gertrude Stein had owned, as well as the portrait of her by Picabia that now hangs on the wall in the Library.

The Schlesinger Library at Radcliffe wrote me an informative letter about Stein materials they have on file. Robert Miller of the Indiana University Library and the reference staff at the Monroe County Public Library were also most cooperative in finding important books and articles for my use. I wish to thank Donald Sutherland, an astute Stein scholar, for an enlightening letter about one aspect of Gertrude Stein's life. In Italy, through the friendly offices of Bernard Perry, nephew of Bernard Berenson, I was welcomed to I Tatti, Berenson's villa (now the Harvard Center for Italian Renaissance Studies) by the acting director, Mason Hammond, and graciously given permission by Dr. C. von Anrep of Milano to examine Stein letters in the archive at I Tatti, most of which were written to the Berensons by Leo Stein.

We were hospitably received at Bilignin, the "dream

house" that Gertrude Stein rented for so many happy summers, by the owner, Mme Gabriel Putz, and her son and daughter-in-law. We spent a pleasant afternoon seeing the handsome house and gardens and visiting with Mme Putz, who as a young woman had known Gertrude Stein and remembered her well. I am grateful, too, to our old friend M. Yvon Bizardel, who reminisced about the many calls that he as a young man had made on Gertrude Stein in her apartment in Paris, enjoying good talk and tea with her and Alice Toklas. From the house we were visiting in Mougins, our kind hostess, Mlle Odette Bornand, directed us to the site of Picasso's well-guarded and tree-shaded house, Notre Dame de Vie, and we caught a glimpse, too, of the house of another artist friend of Stein's, Picabia. It was from Mougins that we made an excursion to spend a day at the Picasso Museum in Antibes.

Good friends in America were helpful in many ways, among them Theodore Bowie, who generously let me use his personal letter signed "Gtde Stein"; Lander MacClintock, who was tireless in collecting useful Stein references; and many others, including A. D. Emmart, I. J. Kapstein, Onya Latour, E. Long, Kenneth McCutchan, Carol and Richard Moody, Elizabeth Pumphrey, Jean Richmond, Elizabeth Cady Saler, and Ruth Sonneborn, who took the time to give me interviews and made gifts or loans of treasured materials by or about the Steins.

Heartfelt appreciation goes to Richard Cameron, my brother, who on severe wintry days in Cambridge persisted on my behalf until with the help of Mrs. Frank Sander, a resident, he found the small brass number "64" which identified the house that Gertrude Stein lived in as a student. The number had long been overlooked because it was no longer used as an address and was on a side door to a large house on Buckingham Street that bore an entirely different number at the front.

Finally I want to mention my husband, William E. Wilson, who took time out from his own writing of a novel to go with me on research trips, not merely as escort but frequently as invaluable interpreter, translator, and photographer. At home when I had spells of absent-mindedness or outbursts of either despair or elation in my attempts to capture on paper Gertrude Stein's complicated life and personality, my husband always suffered these with rare good humor and with complete understanding. I thank him most of all.

Then when any of us were named we were named after some one who is already dead, after all if they are living the name belongs to them so any one can be named after a dead one, so there was a grandmother she was dead and her name not an easy one began with G so my mother preferred it should be an easy one so they named me Gertrude Stein. All right that is my name.

GERTRUDE STEIN: *Everybody's Autobiography*

They named me GERTRUDE STEIN

ONE

There may have been times in her life when Gertrude Stein wished that she weren't so large. Not of course as an infant in Allegheny, Pennsylvania, where she was petted and adored as her father's "perfect baby" and "little dumpling." Nor when she was a toddler taken by the family to Vienna and then to Paris, hugged and spoiled by her parents and her older brothers and sister, who teasingly called her their "round little pudding." And certainly not when many years later, in Paris again as a grown woman, she was sought out by Picasso, Lipchitz, Jo Davidson, and other artists who wanted to capture her large magnificence on canvas or in bronze.

But as a growing girl in California, as a short and too heavy adolescent, there must have been times when she wished she looked more like other girls her age. Even though her eager smile, her large dark eyes and infectious laugh made friends for her, didn't she sometimes look wistfully at her friends, envying their slender grace and the ease with which they danced, flirted, and attracted boys?

If so, she seldom if ever admitted it. She knew that she was too fat, that she looked different. But she also knew that she was different in more important ways and she grew to take pride in these differences. She discovered in school that her mind was quicker than those of her friends, that her feelings of both joy and despair were certainly more intense, that her constant curiosity about what people were really like was more absorbing—and that what she herself was really like and what she would become were of the greatest importance. Now was important only to herself, but someday, she vowed, Gertrude Stein would be important to the world too.

In the meantime she could always count on her brother Leo as best friend and close companion. He was only two years older than she and they did everything together. Gertrude adored him and thought him the cleverest and most interesting boy she knew or ever would know. Together they had much that set them apart not only from their friends but from the others in their family as well. They were the two youngest, they were the only ones who indoors or out devoured books, who almost worshipped the bright California sun, and who talked away the miles as they took long long walks up into the mountains together. They talked about everything—well, almost everything: the books they had read, the plants and creatures they saw on their hikes, and the various ways in which they fully intended to become famous when they were grown up.

There were a few things they did not talk about. Gertrude kept to herself some of her innermost feelings and questions about life, about death. She sometimes wondered if Leo, too, for all his talk, might have a few secret thoughts of his own. But for the most part they chattered constantly and freely about almost every subject under the bright sun.

There was one subject they both skittishly backed away from. That was because it made them "feel funny," Gertrude said. It was the accidental discovery that their father and mother, Daniel and Amelia Stein, had not planned to have them at all. Five children, that's what their parents wanted and that's what they had. There

THEY NAMED ME GERTRUDE STEIN

was Michael, the oldest, a smart one—nine years older than Gertrude, quite grown up and going off east to college. Simon, the extremely fat one, was next—gentle, gluttonous, and not very bright. And Bertha, the sister who had nothing interesting or special about her at all.

There were two other Stein children who had died. If they hadn't, Gertrude learned, she and Leo wouldn't even be alive, for she and her brother were merely substitutes for the two dead children. It was enough to make anyone feel funny, especially Gertrude. What if she hadn't been born on February 3, 1874; what if she had never been born at all! But here she was; she was alive, very much alive, and already eager to make her life so full that some day, like the California sun, she would not only attract and warm but would dazzle everyone. How? As yet she had no idea.

She admitted that Leo was much better at everything than she was! One time—Gertrude remembered that she was about eight years old, although it may have been later—Leo said, "Let's write our own plays." They had both been reading Shakespeare and other Elizabethan drama. Leo dashed off a play full of blood-and-thunder action, swordplay, and heroic speeches. Gertrude got as far in her play as writing stage directions for a scene that was to be full of dialogue. "Here the courtiers make witty remarks," she wrote. But after chewing on her pencil, unable to think of any remarks witty enough to put on paper, she gave up the whole idea of trying to write like Shakespeare. It seemed sadly obvious to her that when she became famous it would not be as a playwright.

She couldn't draw or paint either, the way Leo could. As a child taking lessons in a drawing class, she and the others were told to go home, draw a cup and saucer, and bring the sketches back for the next lesson. The child with the best drawing would be given a medal to take home to keep for a week.

Her mother's dining-room cabinet was filled with precious porcelain brought back from France and Austria when the Steins had lived there on one of their father's extensive business trips. Carefully, Gertrude removed the cup and saucer she thought the prettiest and set them up on the table by her sketch pad. She had no idea how to start her drawing; so Leo hovered over her, making suggestions. Finally, in despair over her ineptness, he took the paper and pencil, made a quick clever sketch, and gave it to his grateful sister.

She was awarded the prize and triumphantly carried off the medal, intending to give it to Leo to keep for the week. After all, he was the one who had earned it. But on the way home she lost it. Not daring to go back the following week and face the instructor or other pupils without the coveted medal, she abruptly gave up her art career. It seemed clear that the future fame she dreamed of would not be hers as an artist of great renown.

What then? Gertrude consoled herself with the thought that there was plenty of time yet in which to discover how to win glory. Meanwhile, she would keep on reading books, devouring books and talking about them to Leo after school or in the summers as they wandered in the California hills together, munching bread when they were hungry and drinking from a mountain stream when they were thirsty.

TWO

It wasn't much fun for the twelve-year-old Gertrude and the fourteen-year-old Leo staying at home in their big house in Oakland now that their mother was either silent or complaining all the time. It was no fun to be under the watchful eyes of the constantly changing housekeepers, governesses, and cooks. It wasn't any fun either to be with their brother Simon, who was only interested in raiding the well-stocked ice box and kitchen cupboards, even occasionally devouring an entire pudding planned for the family dinner. Gertrude loved good food but she looked with disdain on his greedy gobbling. It was no fun to be with their sister Bertha either, for she never had anything interesting to say when she was awake, and at night in the room she shared with Gertrude she ground her teeth in the most annoying way.

Worst of all, Gertrude felt, was bracing herself against their father's evening return from his office across the bay in San Francisco. Daniel Stein's mood was completely unpredictable. If he had a good day with his cable-car company, he was inclined to be jolly and gather all his reluctant children about him after supper to play a game of cards. But that was exasperating because, while he was often too impatient to finish the game himself, he always insisted that the young people play it through to the boring end.

At dinner he often introduced the latest food fad. One

year for a long while he would not allow any meat at the table. He always insisted that the children clean their plates to the very last scrap of food. This was no hardship for Gertrude, who was usually hungry and enjoyed the good dishes prepared by their excellent cook. She even loved spinach. Leo had trouble sometimes. He detested livid orange carrots and pallid yellow turnips; in fact, he said they made him ill. When finally convinced of this, his father usually permitted Leo to omit those two obnoxious vegetables. But once when there was company at the table, Mr. Stein, ignoring his former dispensation, loudly insisted that Leo eat every chunky carrot and every slice of turnip on his plate. On choking them down, the boy became violently ill and had to rush from the room, not to return to the table.

Then there was their father's frequent evening quizzing of his brood. He never read books himself, but he took intense if spasmodic interest in their education. What had they learned in school that day? How did the music lessons go? How long had Leo practiced on his violin? Did Gertrude spend a full hour at the piano? Was she neglecting her schoolwork by doing all this outside reading?

In many ways Gertrude resented her father and his strict domination of the family. But she couldn't help admiring his bigness, his driving ambition, his restless energy that led him from one big undertaking to another, that had led him from trade in wool on the east coast, to the import-export business in Europe, and now to management and the vice-presidency in a cable-car company.

Gertrude was glad that he fully relished life here in the West, for she herself loved living in California. She liked riding the ferry across the bay when they went to the libraries or museums in the city. She enjoyed being

THEY NAMED ME GERTRUDE STEIN

wrapped in the early gray fogs, then soaking up the hot sun, cooling off in the sudden rains. She loved her long walks with Leo up into the mountains. Perhaps most of all, she delighted in getting to know every inch of their ten-acre place, where she could watch all kinds of growing things, plants and animals. Where she could pick and eat the fruit right off the trees in their own orchard. Where she could hide in a hollow with a book and pretend not to hear when someone called and called her to come into the house. Where at night she and Leo and the young people from the small houses nearby could run and play noisy games out of earshot of their parents.

But one night, when she and Leo slipped back into the house all hot and disheveled, their father confronted them. "What were you doing tonight out there running wild all over the place?"

Gertrude pushed back her thick dark hair, tried hastily to smooth her rumpled dress, while Leo answered that they had just been playing hide and seek with the neighbor boys and girls; they didn't even leave the home place. Gertrude added that they just played in the orchard.

Her father was suddenly angry. In the orchard! Didn't Gertrude know that girls shouldn't play with boys out in the orchard at night! Certainly not a daughter of his! Here she was, twelve years old—goodness knows what might happen to her. And Leo! Leo should take better care of her than to let her go hiding in the dark. What was a big brother for if not to see to it that his own sister was safe at home? After tonight Gertrude was not to leave the house. She was to stay home after dark. Was that clear?

It was quite clear. So the next evening Leo went out by himself while Gertrude stayed in her room, a book propped up before her, wondering as she turned the pages what would happen to her some night if one of the boys caught her all alone hiding behind one of the fruit trees.

Would it be something like the time when she was much younger and one little boy, finding her alone, said that he wanted her to do loving with him? When he pulled up her skirt Gertrude didn't understand what he wanted her to do. He began trying to feel her in places that had always before been private when she undressed in her room at home. Gertrude was a little afraid and confused, wanting him to stop, a little excited and daring, wanting him to go on. But she was more afraid and confused than daring. The boy, finding her uncooperative, soon stopped, and after that time he let her alone.

Now that she was twelve and playing hide and seek with the bigger boys, if something like that happened again, how would she feel about it? What would she do? Would she be more daring, encouraging the boy to do what he wanted to? Tonight, as vague imaginings crowded in on her, Gertrude's mind and heart were in a tumult.

A few nights later, when her father seemed to have forgotten all about his stern command, Gertrude began slipping out again after Leo, running and hiding silently, breathlessly, behind a tree or in the high grass, then running free to home base, shrieking with excited laughter. She was half relieved, half sorry that nothing ever seemed to happen to her.

Now Gertrude found she had another subject that she couldn't talk about to anyone—not even to Leo. She kept her vague fears and longings to herself, not really understanding what it was she feared, what it was she longed for.

THEY NAMED ME GERTRUDE STEIN

THREE

Gertrude and Leo continued to be best friends and to talk about almost everything under the California sun. That summer the Stein family were spending their vacation weeks near the town of St. Helena in Napa County. A group excursion was planned to Etna Springs, twenty miles away by horse-drawn stage. The Springs attracted older people, who drank the mineral waters for their health, while the young looked forward to swimming vigorously in the cold waters and being allowed to go down into the mines to watch Chinese laborers working quicksilver.

Their father suggested that since Gertrude and Leo were so fond of hiking and so proud of their ability to cover more miles on foot than anyone else, why didn't they walk the twenty steep miles to the Springs? The rest of them would wait and take the stage as usual.

Gertrude and Leo accepted the challenge with glee. Twenty miles! It would be a history-making walk. They were indignant when their father ventured to guess that by the time the two reached the half-way mark, they would be so footsore and weary that they would be glad to give up and be rescued by the passing stage. So that there would be no temptation, they resolved to set out early on Sunday, a day when the stage wasn't even running. The rest of the party could come up on Monday as planned. Then they'd see! The two marathon walkers would be at the Springs hotel to welcome them.

Before daylight Sunday morning the eager hikers slipped out of the house with the gear they had carefully collected the night before. Leo and Gertrude were awed by the blue-black dome of the sky arching over them and the brilliance of the stars hanging down from the sky, each looking like the separate world it must be. They spoke in hushed voices, for everything in their own familiar world seemed strangely unfamiliar—the big stars, the quiet, the air crisp and cool, while under foot and all around them the pine needles gave out their spicy scent.

It was after sunrise when they reached the first mountain grade and settled down to a steady pace for the long hot climb. Gertrude carried the small satchel filled with food for their roadside picnics. Leo toted his shotgun in case they encountered any game, large or small, that would test his marksmanship. The road that wound up the canyon was covered with thick layers of dry dust that swirled about their feet.

Coming to a small weedy pond by the roadside, Leo stopped abruptly. Gertrude too saw what he had discovered—a bird unlike any they had ever seen, perched on a small island off the bank. While Gertrude stood stock still, Leo took careful aim, fired, and the bird fell over dead. Good shot! Scrambling down to retrieve the bird, Leo stepped on the little island only to find it wasn't an island at all but just some fragile weeds that promptly gave way. He found himself standing in the brackish water up to his waist. The bird had disappeared in the tangle of weeds. Disgusted and dripping, Leo scrambled back up the bank, picked up his gun, and started marching on up the road. Gertrude hurried after

THEY NAMED ME GERTRUDE STEIN

him. Now, as he kicked up dust, it clung to his wet shoes and socks and caked his pants.

With every mile the road grew steeper, the sun hotter. Usually Gertrude couldn't get enough sun, but today it soon became torture. Gertrude's long hair grew more tangled and her perspiring face streaked with dirt. Once in a long while, a farmer in a clattering wagon stopped to offer the bedraggled pair a lift, but they staunchly resisted temptation and declined.

They did stop for an early lunch of fruit and bread and a short rest under a madroña tree. They relaxed in the shade of this evergreen and, before they started off again, almost simultaneously had the same idea. They broke off some of the cool madroña leaves and, putting them under their hats, arranged them to fan out over their faces to protect their eyes and parched skin from the sun's fierce glare.

Refreshed, Gertrude and her brother took to the road again, chattering about the birds they saw, the trees they passed, wishing for more variety. They warned each other about the brilliant red poison oak that they knew could send them to a bed of pain for a week if they so much as brushed against it.

Rounding a steep bend, they stopped abruptly when they saw a jack rabbit sitting in the middle of the road, looking at them impudently with unblinking eyes, his long ears pointing toward them. At once Gertrude stood still, while Leo the hunter tried to load his gun. In his hurry he jammed the cartridge so that it would neither go all the way in nor come back out. The rabbit watched all this with an inquisitive air. Gertrude hardly breathed, she was so afraid the creature would lope away.

Finally, after trying in vain to tug the cartridge out with his teeth, Leo succeeded in cutting it out with his knife. Gertrude stayed as still as a stone. Just as her brother was putting in a new cartridge, the rabbit whisked his tail, twitched his ears, and disappeared into the shrub-like manzanita at the side of the road. What bad luck!

Later, though, Leo was successful in shooting two rabbits, a large woodpecker, and a squirrel. He and Gertrude strung their quarry along the gun and carried it between them, each holding one end. They plodded on. How far had they come on their twenty-mile journey? They did not know. All they knew was that the gun, the dead creatures, the satchel were getting heavier and heavier; the high sun was getting hotter; they were growing tireder, their feet were more leaden every minute. Never had they walked so far, on such a steep and dusty climb, on such a blistering hot day. They confessed to each other that they almost wished they had accepted one of those rides they had so firmly refused.

Soon another farmer rattled up beside them, pulled his mules up short, and urged them to climb aboard. Feebly protesting, they looked at each other, then without a word of further apology gratefully climbed into the wagon. What bliss it was to watch the scenery flow past them as they were carried higher and higher into the hills, watching the Napa Valley with its vineyards disappear completely below them in a haze of heat and the summits above them come more and more clearly into view.

The jolly farmer, learning of their original resolution to walk every foot of the way to the still-far-distant Springs, teased them by asking them every few miles if they didn't want to get off and walk. By now Gertrude and Leo both had dumped their pride overboard and were perfectly willing to accept the farmer's jokes along with the ride. Finally, coming close to their destination,

THEY NAMED ME GERTRUDE STEIN

the two asked to be let out, stiffly climbed down from the rescue wagon, presented the driver with their dead squirrel as payment, shouldered their load once more, and set off on the last long mile to the Springs hotel. It didn't bother them a bit that they could hear their friendly driver's laughter echoing back from the next hill.

Only a mile to go now, but the rabbits and even the woodpecker grew unbearably heavy and were jettisoned by the roadside without regret. Finally, in a last energetic spurt, the two hikers panted up the steps of the hotel piazza just as the dinner bell was ringing.

When curious people crowded around them with questions, Gertrude and Leo just said that before sunrise that morning they set out to walk the whole distance, that their family and the others would not be coming until the next day's stage. What an enthusiastic welcome the bedraggled pair were given! Everyone on the porch was so delighted and impressed that no one would listen when the hikers made feeble attempts to explain that they had accepted a lift for almost the last half of the way.

So Gertrude and Leo gave up protesting and enjoyed every minute of their triumph as they were swept into the dining room for a restoring midday feast. Of course they were on hand next morning to greet the laggard family who had ridden the twenty miles in the horse-drawn stage.

A history-making walk? Perhaps not history, Gertrude granted; history was fact. But at least a legend, fiction mixed with fact—a legend of the two youngsters who made twenty steep miles on foot in a half day's time. It wasn't exactly the kind of fame that Gertrude dreamed of having some day, but at least it gave her and Leo a brief and heady place in the limelight.

FOUR

Gertrude often found her parents exasperating in their lack of understanding. She knew that her father was disappointed in her. His "perfect baby" of long ago had grown into an awkward overweight adolescent daughter who didn't do what he wanted her to. He would demand to know why she wasn't trying to learn to sew, to cook, to be domestic, like the girls who lived in the smaller, poorer houses near them. At times Gertrude would merely sulk under his criticism. Sometimes she flared up at him. How could he expect her to learn to do those things when he always had a cook to rule over their big kitchen, a seamstress who did all the sewing and mending for them, various other women he paid to scrub and clean and polish their big house from top to bottom!

And her mother? Her little mother who showed scant interest in anything outside her home, who seemed content to live in the shadow of her rich, successful husband, who for herself only wanted nice children, a well-run house, a good table, and simple but expensive clothing to wear.

While Gertrude knew her mother loved her, she also knew that she must be disappointed in her tomboyish daughter who didn't much care what she wore or how often she snagged her skirts or muddied her boots or

16

lost her umbrella; a daughter who was too big and who flung herself into chairs and couldn't seem to remember how to be prim and proper like the young lady her mother hoped she would become. Gertrude thought it sad that her mother never responded to the freedom of unconventional life in the West. Instead, she tried in her household to continue the decorum and even elegance that she had been used to in her own girlhood in Baltimore. Worst of all, why was her mother always more interested in how her children looked and behaved than in how they felt and in what they were thinking?

As her health failed, she could no longer manage the household or the servants. She could no longer control her independent family. As her brood grew big around her, their mother seemed to shrink in body and spirit. Gertrude tried to remember that it was because her mother was ill that she grew more and more fretful. But it was hard not to be impatient with her querulousness. She even wished that her mother would give way occasionally to the quick stubborn little bursts of temper that she used to have. At least then she would assert herself, show that she still was somebody, a person to be listened to, taken into account.

Gertrude sometimes thought that it was from her mother as well as from her father that she had inherited her own quick temper, her own way of declaring her independence. All her life she vividly remembered the first time when as a little girl she had asserted herself, letting her anger boil up inside her until it spilled over.

She was on her way home from the first grade at school with other children in her neighborhood, carrying an umbrella for a friend after a rain and trying to keep up with the others when they began to run ahead along the muddy street. She struggled desperately to catch up to them, but they ran too fast for her and soon disappeared, leaving her far behind, tearful and angry. She was angry with the umbrella for getting in her way as she tried to run. She was furious with the girls for deserting her. She was angry at being left behind and all alone. As her anger grew, churning violently inside her, she cried out, "I will throw the umbrella in the mud." No one heard her. But again and again she made her threat to the empty street. "I will throw the umbrella in the mud!" At last, in one final burst of anger and desperation, she hurled the umbrella from her and cried out in bitter triumph, "I have throwed the umbrella in the mud!" And with this act of defiance her anger left her and she ran home, leaving the umbrella behind in the muddy street.

Even though no one saw or heard her that day, Gertrude felt for years afterward that she had proved something to herself, that she had shown she was a person to be reckoned with. She was somebody. And though later there were troubled times when she lost that feeling, she never lost it completely or permanently as her mother was now losing it—that feeling of being important to oneself.

As her mother grew weaker and she was discovered to have cancer, her father moved the family from the big place that required so much supervision to a much smaller house in town. Here the mother had less house to worry about, was closer to doctors, and the children closer to school. The father also hinted that business was not good; his latest scheme had apparently fallen through. For a while they must all be careful about spending money for anything but necessities.

Young Gertrude was desolate. She wanted her mother to get the best care, of course. She didn't particularly

THEY NAMED ME GERTRUDE STEIN

want to be nearer school, and money meant nothing to her so long as she and Leo could buy books for themselves. To them, books were necessities not luxuries. But she desperately missed their old place out on the edge of town, surrounded by high rose hedges, marked by rows of eucalyptus trees. That was the place where she could hide out in solitude when she was in the mood, the place where she and Leo together could have long talks, safely away from their parents' eyes and ears.

Now they had only an ordinary yard. Gertrude felt that they were all crowded together under the smaller roof in the little house filled with sickness and worry— and death.

Gertrude was fourteen when her mother died.

For a long time she had been brooding about the idea of death and about her own death that was sure to happen some day. It wasn't so much that she was afraid of dying as that she was frightened by the idea of dissolving into nothingness, of not existing after death. She wanted to keep on living somehow, somewhere.

Was there a future life? She couldn't find a definite answer anywhere—not in Sabbath School or in the synagogue services that the Steins sometimes attended, where life on earth and not in the hereafter seemed important. She couldn't find the answer in the public school, where most of her schoolmates came from families that practiced a different religion. Nor was it in any of the books Gertrude read so avidly. Surely the Bible would have the answer—if not the Old Testament, then the New.

Fearfully but eagerly she read the Book of Revelation, but discovered little promise of eternal life. When she found phrases about the book of life, waters of life, the tree of life, the crown of life, and even the phrase "living for ever and ever," the words seemed to her to refer to the life of God on his throne and that of his mighty angels, and as a reward for those martyrs of centuries ago, not to a future life for others. Certainly not for her, a troubled young girl who was certain to die some day.

FIVE

After the mother's death the Stein household became completely disorganized. Sister Bertha at eighteen and nineteen years of age tried ineffectually to have regular meals for the family, but she was scatterbrained and was given little cooperation from the others.

When Michael, the eldest, was graduated from Johns Hopkins University and came back to California, he lived his own life across the bay in San Francisco. He worked at a good job in the cable-car company that his father managed.

Simon continued to eat constantly between meals, so that it made little difference to him if something was formally called the supper hour and the table was set or not. Gertrude and Leo refused to be tied to dull routine and came and went as they pleased.

Mr. Stein, now gloomy, irritable, and often withdrawn, was given to sudden and unpredictable flashes of anger when he tried to get his heedless family back into line.

In rebellion against their father's dictatorship, Gertrude and Leo stood up to his verbal attacks or, whenever they could, avoided them altogether, going their own way, finding what pleasure they could away from the depressing household. They still went on long walks in all sorts of weather, but now that they felt they were growing up, being well into their teens, they often turned to the city for entertainment. They rode the ferry to San

Francisco, where they not only haunted the libraries and the museums but went to the theater together.

Gertrude was delighted by opera and some of the plays she saw, but she was depressed and even disturbed by others. Action on the stage was very real to her, embroiling her and pulling her along too rapidly from one emotional response to another. *Dr. Jekyll and Mr. Hyde* as acted by the great Richard Mansfield threw her into a panic so that she had to leave the theater long before the last act. It seemed to her that she, too, often experienced such an inner struggle between her better and worse selves. She spent several sleepless nights fearing that, like the hero-villain, she herself might be going mad.

But when Sarah Bernhardt, the famous French actress, came to town, Gertrude watched her with fascinated attention. The Divine Sarah's acting in *La Dame aux Camélias, Jeanne d'Arc*, and other plays was so foreign, her voice was so golden, and not only her speech but her appearance and gestures, her thin expressive arms were all so *French* that Gertrude's eyes and ears were absorbed by the spectacular performance, while her heart remained untroubled by the conflicting emotions that often tore her to pieces in the theater.

She couldn't understand many of the lines as declaimed on the stage, but she remembered enough French from her year with the family in Paris when she was a child to feel at home in the rhythms and inflections of the language as she heard it while sitting in the darkened theater in San Francisco.

Anyone and anything French always attracted Gertrude's lively curiosity and interest—the French M. and Mme Henry with five children who lived near them and spoke French at home, the books by Jules Verne that she read, the French plays and operas that she went to see with Leo. Even her first overwhelming experience with art, she remembered, was when as an eight-year-old she had found herself standing in the center of a platform completely surrounded by a huge cyclorama of the Battle of Waterloo that was on exhibit in San Francisco.

At first Gertrude had walked slowly along with Leo, who was interested in the mural not only as art but to discover for himself whether or not the historic details of the battle were depicted accurately. Leo often thought he would be a famous historian some day and so had memorized endless lists of dates and facts. Delightedly he pointed out to Gertrude the amazing detail in the panorama—everything from the field that looked sodden with rain, through the battle with its gun carriages, the smoking cannons, the proper regimental colors, horses rearing, men dying, and the final defeat of the stunned Napoleon riding off in his old green coat, protected only by a few loyal mounted grenadiers.

Gertrude was impressed by Leo's knowledge of the battle down to the last detail as pictured here. Then, standing alone for a while in the middle of the platform, she felt the mural as a work of art sweeping around her. She was struck for the first time that while a painting might look like the out-of-doors, there was an important difference: the outdoors is never a flat surface, it is made up of air, and a painting is always a flat surface even when there is an attempt in the picture to imitate air. Discovering this simple but basic difference made painting seem new and exciting to the young Gertrude as she stood there surrounded by the cyclorama of the Battle of Waterloo—as big as all outdoors. She must tell Leo of her discovery sometime, though he would probably say he had known that all along.

Some years later, another canvas to capture Gertrude's intense interest was Millet's "Man with the Hoe." Here again it was a French painting that absorbed her. For the first time she wanted to own a reproduction of an oil painting as much as she had always wanted to own books. With excitement, she bought a photograph of the painting and showed it to Michael, her indulgent eldest brother. "What is it?" he asked, puzzled by his young sister's enthusiasm.

"Man with the Hoe," she answered.

His only comment was, "That's a hell of a hoe."

But to Gertrude it was not only a picture of a French peasant working the French earth with just that kind of hoe; the photograph reminded her of Millet's original oil painting, and that was important to her. Leo was the only one who understood how much a painting could mean to her because paintings meant much to him too.

In spite of going to plays, enjoying pictures, reading books, and in spite of having Leo as good companion, Gertrude at fifteen and sixteen was often moody and lonely. The plays sometimes upset her, the exhibition pictures came and went, she wept over the sorrows of book characters that she understood better than she understood herself. There was no one she could ask about the mysteries of life, of sex that troubled her. Soon Leo would be going off to college; she dreaded that, for then she would feel utterly abandoned. She had no real confidante, no other close friend, not even in school.

Her high-school classes were such a bore to her that she was often tempted to drop out altogether. She felt that she was learning far more in her outside reading than she was in school. The public library meant far more to her than high school ever did. Her only fear was that some day she might have read everything in the library; then where would there be any books left for her to discover?

The only activity in school that delighted her was the

THEY NAMED ME GERTRUDE STEIN

diagramming of sentences. The precision and logic of putting parts of speech where they belonged was as satisfying to her as taking a complicated puzzle apart and easily putting it together again. But diagramming sentences took up only a small part of the long and tedious school days.

While she sometimes had good times with her classmates after school, she found none who was interested in the things that interested her. They all belonged to the school's Lend a Hand Society and eagerly vied with each other in reporting every week how they had lent a helping hand to someone in the family. Gertrude and Leo thought it silly to brag about being do-gooders. They themselves never could have any helping hand of their own to report even if they had wanted to, for each member of their erratic family went his own way and never looked for any help from the others, certainly not from the two youngest.

One morning, when Gertrude was seventeen, they discovered that their father was completely beyond asking for or receiving any help of any kind from anyone. Gertrude and the others were not at first concerned when he failed to come down for breakfast at his usual time; it was rarely that the entire family sat down to a meal together. But when it was past time for their father to catch the ferry to go to work, they were puzzled and uneasy. One after another they called him and knocked on his locked door. There was no answer.

Alarmed now, Leo ran outside, climbed in through the open window of Daniel Stein's room, and discovered that their father had died in his bed. It was the quiet end of a turbulent life.

Now Michael became head of the family.

SIX

"Mike," as Gertrude and Leo called their twenty-six-year-old brother and guardian, was usually calm and always kind and conscientious in his care of the young orphans. But more important to them was that, while he did not always understand and often protested their somewhat unusual interests, he tolerated them and indulgently gave the two an allowance that allowed Gertrude and Leo to buy the prints, books, and theater and opera tickets that they felt they could not live without.

Mike, though he did not like business, was proving himself a good businessman. He not only took on the debts left by his father but brought to a triumphant conclusion one of his father's big unfulfilled schemes—that of persuading C. P. Huntington, the Central Pacific magnate, to buy Mr. Stein's franchise in the Omnibus Cable Company, thus carrying through his father's long-dreamed-of scheme for consolidating the street railways.

Because of his astute business sense, Mike was at first made branch manager and eventually manager of the entire system. The investments he made were so shrewd that Mike knew the young Steins, if they lived modestly, could all count on small but steady incomes for years to come. This relieved his greatest anxiety, for he feared that his young charges were too impractical ever to earn their own living.

"Living modestly" meant moving to a house in San Francisco with Mike as head of the household; Bertha trying inadequately to manage the domestic scene; Simon, his pockets full of candy, working at the routine job of cable-car grip man; Leo, the acknowledged intellectual of the family, attending college classes at nearby Berkeley.

And Gertrude? Gertrude, who had long since quit high school, having had more than enough of the uninspiring instruction there, still read avidly any book she could lay her hands on, took singing and piano lessons, and even for a brief time had a beau with whom she played duets. The young man was different from the uncouth grade-school boys Gertrude had known. He planned to go to college, he knew something about music, and while Gertrude thought he wasn't, *couldn't* be, so bright or interesting as Leo, still he seemed to understand her language.

They enjoyed many evenings at home together, talking, singing, and playing the piano. Gertrude, sitting heavily on the piano bench, was vivacious—her eyes shone, her pleasing voice sang out joyfully, her surprisingly delicate hands roamed easily over the keys, her talk was animated and entertaining. She bloomed into loveliness. But when the young man went off to college, she didn't hear from him again. Gertrude sadly concluded that she really hadn't interested him; apparently she wasn't really interesting to anyone. She felt very much alone and very lonely.

She desperately needed friends, one real friend. While Mike was busy earning a living and Leo was absorbed in his classes at Berkeley, Gertrude sat alone in a corner of the public library surrounded by books—books that seemed to have lost their savor, books that were dusty, inanimate. They had no answers to all the questions she kept asking about herself. After all, musty books were no real substitute for life.

One day when a funeral procession passed in the street outside the library windows, she was moved to tears and despair by the stirring notes of Chopin's funeral march, by the sight of the long black hearse, by the small pathetic figures following on foot. Was death the only answer? What had become of her childhood joy in the outdoors, in books, in people? What had become of her childhood dreams of fame? If only something would happen, something to break these wild dark moods that possessed her, something to change her dreary solitary existence.

Something did happen. Whether Mike, sensing her inner despair, maneuvered the invitation from Baltimore that would change her whole outlook, or whether the invitation came spontaneously from relatives there who took pity on bachelor Mike's trying to care for the orphaned family in San Francisco, Gertrude never knew for certain. The important thing was that the invitation did come.

Their mother's sister, Aunt Fannie Bachrach, affectionately urged that the two girls Bertha and Gertrude come to live with them in Baltimore. There was plenty of room in their big house; the girls should get to know their cousins and aunts and uncles who lived in various homes in that Eastern city. All would warmly welcome the two who had lived so far away from the family circle for too long.

Gertrude was eager for a change—this or any other. But she wasn't much pleased over the prospect of Bertha's going. Bertha was never a good companion. What about Leo? She couldn't bear to have a whole continent between them. It was decided that if he wanted to, Leo could transfer to a college in the East,

THEY NAMED ME GERTRUDE STEIN

Harvard perhaps. His cousin Fred Stein was a student there. Leo could spend vacations in Baltimore and even come down from Cambridge for an occasional weekend. Gertrude rejoiced when Leo enthusiastically fell in with that plan. Harvard! There he would find the stimulating atmosphere he craved.

Now Gertrude's spirits rose dizzily at the prospect of the new venture, a long and exciting train journey all the way across the country, a whole new family circle in a completely different city, new faces, new friends—all this, and Leo not too far away to share his own new experiences with her.

At the last minute Gertrude found it a wrench to be leaving California, with its sunshine, its mountains, its valleys and vineyards. California would always be a part of her. It was a wrench, too, to leave Mike, hard-working Mike who had tried to understand her. Simon? Poor Simon! But he had what he wanted, a lowly job that gave him a chance to talk to people, passing out candy to the children and cigars to the men who rode the cable cars. He was content.

Gertrude did not spend much time in brooding, however, or much time in packing. She packed books because they were essential to her, but when it came to clothes, she took only what she considered indispensable, including her favorite battered old straw hat. While Bertha puttered over the details of her wardrobe—choosing, discarding, changing her mind a dozen times about which hat she should wear with her travel costume—Gertrude was at first impatient, but suddenly burst into delighted laughter. She reminded her sister what had happened to Bertha's hat when their parents had first brought the family west by train a dozen years ago. The two girls, then six and twelve years old, were both wearing beautiful bonnets of red felt that their elegant little mother had purchased for them during their long stay in Europe. Bertha's big hat with its ostrich plume blew out of the open window one day when the train was chugging its way across the vast plains. Hearing her cry of dismay, their resourceful father promptly pulled the emergency cord and stopped the train. While engineer, conductors, and passengers watched in amazement, Daniel Stein jumped off, ran back, picked up the hat, boarded the train again, and presented it to his daughter, hat unharmed, ostrich feather still nodding gracefully. This was one of Gertrude's few happy memories of her father, of his bigness, his boldness, and his occasional impulsive indulgence of his children when they were young.

Now here they were, three of them, practically grown up, boarding the train again, taking the long trip back East, excited at the prospect of the new life ahead. If Gertrude had any qualms about going to relatives whom she could scarcely remember, her uncertainties were completely swallowed up in the warm embracing welcome they all received upon reaching Baltimore.

They lived in the spacious home of Aunt Fannie Bachrach, but other relatives such as their mother's brother Uncle Eph Keyser, the sculptor, and a whole bevy of cheerful voluble aunts were in and out of Aunt Fannie's house to welcome the Westerners and plan numerous entertainments for them in their own substantial, comfortable homes.

If any of this close-knit, hospitable family at first thought Bertha a nonentity, Leo inclined to be an intellectual snob, and Gertrude herself too plump, too ebullient, and too much of a breezy Westerner for their more restrained and carefully ordered lives, they were affectionate enough and courteous enough to hide their feelings. Besides, it was not long before Bertha slipped into her quiet, undemanding niche; Leo charmed the young lady cousins and their friends the Cone sisters, Etta and Claribel, with his gallantry, his wit, and his eloquent enthusiasm over the art he discovered in the Walters Gallery. Gertrude won everyone over with her unaffected, childlike pleasure in and curiosity about everything, from the elegant furnishings and accessories of onyx and crystal in the various family homes to the rows upon rows of Baltimore houses whose marble front steps were scrubbed white in the mornings. Her young cousin, seven-year-old Helen, adored Gertrude's open friendliness, her frequent laugh, her kindly good humor. Her laugh as it rang out in polite drawing rooms was so infectious that hostesses almost forgave her for flinging herself on their delicate sofas. Her unabashed interest in the lives of the servants, both black and white, made her welcome even in the backstairs regions of these well-staffed houses. She reveled in the soft relaxed atmosphere of the city and listened with pleasure to the slow musical voices of the South.

But when Leo went off to Harvard and sent back letters full of the excitement of new studies, classes, friends, and professors, he occasionally stirred in his sister a ripple of envy. If only she were prepared to go to college too, she would be willing to exchange her lazy peaceful life for one like Leo's in the stimulating world of ideas. The only lessons she was taking were polite singing lessons.

Meanwhile, she had become the staunch friend of all the little aunts. One dark night when she was walking some of them to their homes after a gala evening at Aunt Fannie's, a man stepped out menacingly from behind a tree and confronted them all. Gertrude was frightened, but without a moment's hesitation she said to the aunts, "Go on home. I will take care of him!" When with fast-beating heart she turned to face the intruder, he slunk away without a word or gesture.

Another time, when Gertrude was on her way to her singing lesson in a different part of the city, she stopped abruptly as she saw a woman accosting a man on the street. They seemed to know each other. As the woman with flushed face upturned asked the man something, whether in anger or appeal she could not tell, the man struck the woman hard with his umbrella. Gertrude watched the woman hurry away, weeping; then she herself walked on, her emotions in turmoil. Why was the man so violent? What did it all mean? What did the man and woman mean to each other? Was it love or hate or both?

Gertrude felt that she had to know more, learn more about men and women, about life. She felt that while she was happy here, she was too sheltered, too protected, living as she did with her gentle guardian relatives. Why would a man strike a woman with his umbrella? Obviously, he had not wanted her to approach him in public. But why?

Somehow in ways that Gertrude could not explain even to herself, the picture of that strange and violent encounter finally helped crystallize her long-dormant desire to go to college. There she would surely learn much about people that she didn't know. She wanted, too, to be near Leo to share his new life.

At Leo's urging and with Mike's consent, Gertrude applied for admission to the Harvard Annex, later called Radcliffe. She had never finished high school and had no diploma, but she knew she was better versed in the English classics than most high-school graduates; she knew no Latin but could read French and German well enough to pass those college-entrance exams. If she had

THEY NAMED ME GERTRUDE STEIN

to know Latin in order to graduate, she could take care of that later.

When the joyful news arrived that she was accepted as a student, Gertrude once again packed up her many books and her few clothes. She clapped her battered straw sailor hat on her head and, after assuring the little aunts that she would be back often to visit them, went off with Leo to Cambridge for the fall term of 1893.

SEVEN

In the beginning, Gertrude found everything about Cambridge strange and exciting. First of all there was the large frame rooming and boarding house at 64 Buckingham Street where she unpacked her books in a room that was to be her home for the next four years. She thought the landlord who sat at the head of the long dining-room table was funny. Did he mean to be funny? Gertrude wasn't sure, since this was her first encounter with Yankee humor. He hated to eat under dim lights and said so. Gertrude chuckled when once he complained that if they had another light as feeble as the one hanging over the table, they would all be in total darkness. His pleasant wife ran the house well and kept a good table, though Gertrude found it odd to have codfish cakes for breakfast, no tomatoes in the milky clam chowder on Fridays, and to have baked beans and brown bread every single Saturday night.

The other young ladies from the Annex who lived there were a new breed to Gertrude—young intellectuals who were bright, angular, extremely earnest, and always ready to discuss ideas but less willing to reveal their feelings. Her always lively curiosity about people was baffled by their New England reserve, which at first she took for unfriendliness. She said once that when she first arrived in Cambridge the only people who smiled at her on the street were the few black children playing there. As she grew to know the girls in her house better, she found them genuinely friendly but seldom without that final wall of reserve.

Here in Cambridge the air itself was different from the soft and languorous air of Baltimore; it was invigorating and had such a nip in it that Gertrude walked with a new briskness the eight or so blocks from her boarding house to her classes in Fay House across from the Cambridge Common and almost in the shadow of the majestic Washington Elm. As she walked, she looked with pleasure on the wide lawns and comfortable old homes, particularly the very old handsome Colonial and Federal houses along Brattle Street with their many-paned windows and with fanlights arching over the front doorways. Autumn came early to Cambridge and Gertrude was intoxicated by the colors in the leafy canopy that curved high over her head and over the walks and the wide streets.

The New England speech that she heard on all sides was so clipped and rapid, so different from the slow musical drawl that had delighted her in Maryland and so different from the frank and open twang that she had known in California that Gertrude had difficulty at first in understanding her fellow students and professors. And that accent! The Harvard Annex—not to be named Radcliffe until her sophomore year—was always referred to as the Ha'v'd Annex; and the Yard, sacred to male students, precincts that no young lady was supposed to enter without an escort, was known to everyone as Ha'v'd Ya'd.

The way students and faculty said things puzzled and amused Gertrude, but *what* they said interested her enormously. She had never been so surrounded by keen and speculative minds, people who argued sometimes brilliantly and usually endlessly over everything from William James's theory of the conscious to everyone's individual idea of the existence of God. Quickly Gertrude learned to enjoy a good argument and she plunged fearlessly into every discussion in classrooms and in the boarding house, where girls gathered in each other's rooms late at night after study hours.

It didn't take long for Gertrude even as a freshman to be recognized as a lively new addition to the student body of two hundred young ladies. She was something different, an original out of that unfamiliar world outside New England. It took a longer time for her fellow students to accept these differences.

Did they think her too fat? Yes. But when they looked directly into her brown eyes they found them sparkling in eager response. Her round face in spite of the heaviness of her body seemed sensitive and vulnerable, appealing in its open-eyed wonder. And although she was far heavier than her thin and angular classmates, she proved that she could out-walk and out-bicycle most of them on their Saturday afternoon excursions into the countryside all the way to and around Fresh Pond.

Did her clothes sometimes look as though she had thrown them on? Definitely. The neatly dressed New Englanders shook their heads over the way her shirtwaists refused to stay tucked in properly under her belts; and her old sailor hat, they said, really ought to be thrown into the fire. In fact, the boarding-house girls good-naturedly conspired to get rid of the faded and battered hat and finally did throw it into the ash barrel. Gertrude just laughed when any of the girls ventured to remark on her wardrobe or her weight.

Was her laugh too frequent and too explosive? Certainly. Sometimes you could hear her a block away. But her laugh was so spontaneous, so contagious, that in the

THEY NAMED ME GERTRUDE STEIN

end none except the most proper Bostonians could resist it.

Did she argue too loudly and too vehemently? Gertrude herself admitted that she did. But others found her talk usually original, always stimulating. The professors who came over to Fay House to repeat their Harvard lectures to the young women of the Annex usually found Miss Stein one of the most responsive of the students, full of eager questions. She showed little of the modest restraint of her New England–bred classmates. In philosophy class under that exciting trio of professors, George Palmer, Santayana, and William James, and in European history, too, she consistently made "A's" and that first year did almost as well in economics and German.

Thanks to Leo, Gertrude soon became a member of the Philosophy Club, where Leo and his friends and now she herself held forth. Later she was elected secretary and helped to plan discussion programs that were meat and drink to her.

But college life was not all books and earnest discussion. The Boston Symphony Orchestra concerts both in Boston and in Sanders Theater in Cambridge became high points in her life. She reveled in being a neighbor on Buckingham Street of the renowned founder of the orchestra, Colonel Henry Lee Higginson, even though he was unaware of her existence.

She followed Leo to exhibits at the Boston Museum of Fine Arts, later helping a friend, Tommy Whittemore, to unpack the newly acquired Chinese art collection there. With Leo she was excited over the prospect of the new Fogg Museum, soon to be built for Harvard's own infant collection of fine arts.

In spite of all these diversions, Gertrude was still beset occasionally by her dark moods. As winter came on, they were as gray and dark as the long hard winter itself. She despaired of ever getting used to the New Englanders' self-contained temperament. She admired their intellectual prowess and their Puritan moral sense, which she felt was really much like her own. But why, oh why, did they have to be so rigid? Why couldn't they relax and be more spontaneous in their relationships with people like herself?

She knew that Leo felt it was their being Jewish that made some of the classmates keep the Steins at arm's length. For once Gertrude did not agree with Leo. She saw other young intellectual Jews who were not looked upon as outsiders. She concluded that the difference was that she and Leo had not grown up in New England; they had not gone to the right prep schools; nobody here had ever heard of the Stein parents and grandparents; nobody here had ever heard of the Stein children before they came to college. Well, they would hear of them, Gertrude resolved. She would see to that!

When the bleakness of the Cambridge winter began to dissolve, Gertrude's moods dissolved too. At last, when spring came, she found the new season a heady delight. Gray skies, dirty snow, and slush gave way to balmier days. The air lost its bite. It gradually filled with the sweet fragrance of lilacs. The sun warmed the coldest of New Englanders. With her friends Gertrude took leisurely walks along the Charles River, watching the colorful boat-club races. They rode their bicycles together out Brattle Street, way out to Fresh Pond with its willows turning from early gold to richer green. She found that even the traditional Harvard indifference gave way, with young men enthusiastically organizing picnics and evening parties on excursion boats in Boston Harbor.

If at times Gertrude was disappointed that a more

personal and romantic attachment did not develop with one of her male companions, she at least had the satisfaction of knowing that Leo's friends were beginning to invite her on outings not just because she was Leo's sister but because she was herself. They obviously enjoyed her company, even though they still looked upon her with some astonishment. She knew that they never entirely got used to her impulsiveness, her heartiness, her way of freely expressing herself—ways that were as natural to her as restraint was to them.

After June exam week she learned that she had triumphantly survived her freshman year, had proved herself one of the top students in her class. Now she even looked forward with enthusiasm to coming back next September. New England was a good place after all.

EIGHT

As a sophomore, Gertrude plunged into two courses that meant much to her. In one she learned more about understanding other people—this was an experimentation class in the psychology lab. The other taught her more about understanding herself; this was a composition course, a writing class that became almost a confessional to her. Here she unburdened herself on paper in the famous English 22 that required a daily theme both from its men students over in the Yard and from the young women at Radcliffe.

When told to write of "something that interests you," Gertrude wrote of herself. Sometimes in her themes she used the first person singular, sometimes she wrote about an unnamed third person, sometimes she described a young woman whom she called Hortense. But first person, third person, Hortense—all of them were really Gertrude.

She wrote about her childhood, of her rebellion against her strong-willed father, of her unusual closeness to her brother. She wrote at length about her sympathy with the West, where people could be free and independent and unconventional. She poured out her feeling for Baltimore and the sunny South, where family, friends, even strangers surrounded one with warm affection, where one could be indolent and fall into delicious daydreams.

She wrote of her early reactions to New England, how

THEY NAMED ME GERTRUDE STEIN

too often its climate and its people seemed to her cold and depressing. In these papers she described herself—or Hortense—as "rather stout," "vehement and fiery," "tremendously moral." Indeed, her continuous struggle between her naturally impulsive nature and her strict moral conscience was the motif underlying many of her compositions.

Her very first theme must have startled the young Harvard graduate, William Vaughn Moody, who read and graded the young ladies' papers. He must have looked a second time at the name Gertrude Stein. She called her theme "In the Red Deeps," a title that Moody recognized as the title of a chapter out of *The Mill on the Floss* by George Eliot, who was apparently Miss Stein's favorite author.

George Eliot's heroine Maggie was shown in constant struggle between her passionate nature and her high moral sense. Gertrude's heroine Hortense was very like her. The theme was partly imaginative and partly introspective, full of melodramatic descriptions of a girl's conflict between her better and worse selves. Even fear of madness came into the theme, and the kind of inner turmoil that had so disturbed Gertrude when younger that she could not bear to watch a performance of *Dr. Jekyll and Mr. Hyde* to the end.

Mr. Moody's astonished but restrained comment on the piece was "Extraordinary." Could it possibly be personal, he asked. If so, it was told in a highly exaggerated manner. If objective, it was surely a study of a morbid psychological state! There was no doubt in the instructor's mind about one feature of Gertrude's papers: they were full of grammatical errors, misspellings, faulty punctuation, and confused point of view. Frequently she was asked to rewrite a theme. But these errors, which were due to lack of training and which gained her a lowly "C" in the course, could not hide the passionate sincerity of her themes.

Another paper she wrote later in the year, intended as the first chapter in a novel, again presents Hortense. Here she is described as "in the full sensuous development of budding womanhood." There are times when Hortense becomes possessed of a "wild impatience" toward the necessity for constant study, rebelling against the endless required reading lists, railing against the remoteness of higher education for women from the realities of life. At such times the only way she can escape herself and calm her rebellious mood, she writes, is to take a long and vigorous walk in the biting cold air.

The last theme she wrote at the end of the year Gertrude called "The Temptation." Again she took the title from *The Mill on the Floss,* except that George Eliot called hers "The Great Temptation." Gertrude's piece was extraordinary in its candid portrayal of a girl's inner struggle between her strict Puritan conscience and her yielding to the temptation of bodily sensation.

Remembering an incident from her Baltimore days, Gertrude again uses Hortense as the character who this time is in a church so filled that many were left standing crowded together in the rear. She allows a man deliberately to lean against her so closely that she knows they both feel a strong stirring of the senses. She is ashamed that she does not move away at once. She realizes that her cousins and her aunt become aware of the shameful contact but she falls so completely under its spell that she refuses to acknowledge her relatives' discreet signals to her to draw away. Her own conscience berates her, her body refuses to listen. Finally a cousin comes to break her away from this intimate involvement. On the way home Hortense denies to them that she was conscious of any wrongdoing. But to herself and in her theme Gertrude is honest enough to admit that she had been both a coward and a liar, for even while despising herself she had indeed yielded to temptation.

Mr. Moody, the reader, again startled by the frankness of the confession, commented that the theme was extremely unpleasant but that it had certain "psychological interest."

"Psychological interest." That was what absorbed Gertrude—interest in people, herself and others. Psychology, that newest branch of philosophy, was the study that Gertrude felt she had been looking for all along. She soon admired and even adored William James, her professor, whose courses she took throughout the rest of her college career.

No one but Leo had ever before awakened in her such hero worship. The fact that Leo, too, revered William James as a brilliant, stimulating teacher only intensified her own devotion. One of the few completely selfless themes that Gertrude wrote in English 22 her sophomore year was a paean of praise for her new hero. "Was life worth living?" she asked. "Yes, a thousand times yes when the world still holds such spirits as Professor James."

In the classroom, William James was amusing and deadly serious in turn, sometimes both at once. He looked something like a shrewd rooster with his long thin face, his prominent beak of a nose, his scraggly beard and coxcomb of hair, and his occasional crows of delight over unexpected responses in class. He was always trying to provoke his students to think for themselves. Gertrude was exhilarated by this approach and her own responses were so original and lively that she was invited by James to join his graduate seminar in psychology and to work under him and Hugo Münsterberg.

She called the students in the lab "a funny bunch" and she thoroughly enjoyed being one of them. They worked singly or in pairs on all kinds of problems. One young man, MacDougall, worked on the phenomenon of religious conversion. Another student busied himself with incubating chickens and studying their actions. There was a Russian who, having hidden an object under a table cover, had other students watch while he snatched away the cloth, revealing a pistol lying there. He must have been disappointed in Gertrude's reaction, which was no reaction at all. Unless a pistol was in the hands of a dangerous person, she maintained, why would the sight of one make anyone jump!

And then there was Leon Solomons. Gertrude was attracted to him first because he had the kind of Jewish and Western friendliness that she felt at ease with. He, too, was from California. As they worked together on various experiments having to do with consciousness, she grew to admire the way his mind worked and to like him more and more. Together they made a good team.

They were to study automatic responses in humans and at first they used each other as subjects. They soon gave up an experiment involving tuning forks, for while Gertrude was very fond of music, neither she nor her partner proved to have a good ear for individual tones. Next, at the suggestion of William James, they made a planchette to use—a small three-cornered board with a pencil for one of its short legs. What would result if one of them lightly held fingers on the board and moved it about while the other read a story aloud to distract him? Eventually they used just pencil and paper in their studies of attention.

Solomons published Gertrude's findings with his under both their names in an article titled "Normal Motor

Automatism." It appeared in a professional journal, *Psychological Review,* in September 1896. This was the first time Gertrude's name had appeared in print and she was pleased. She did not entirely agree with Solomons's conclusions, but she readily acknowledged that Leon, the graduate student, was the major author; her minor contribution was that of an undergraduate.

Striking out on her own, she tested other students who were not trained observers in psychology, thinking they were unprejudiced subjects. She wrote up her results, which Solomons respected, although he criticized the careless way in which she presented them. After he had altered a few of her awkward sentences and freely inserted commas where Gertrude had blithely omitted them, her findings were published in another issue of *Psychological Review* as "Cultivated Motor Automatism." She always considered this her first published work and was enormously pleased to have her own article in print.

Could any of these experiments be said to have resulted in "automatic writing"? Gertrude thought not, saying years later that Solomons and she had always known what they were doing when they tested each other, and unless perhaps they could be hypnotized, which they were not, no students could produce genuine automatic writing under the conditions set up for them in the lab.

Basically, Gertrude found that in experiments on herself or with others, what interested her most and what she wanted to write about was the basic character, the personality, of the individual involved. What people were really like. Their "bottom nature," as she called it, was most important to her and was what influenced their response both in the lab and in life. Were they "nervous, high-strung, imaginative, and strong in concentration" or were they "phlegmatic, passive, weak in concentration"? While Solomons was always the searching scientist, Gertrude was primarily the student of human nature.

There were times when she wished that Leon Solomons would be less scientific and more personal in his awareness of her own responses. She even wrote for composition class an amusingly rueful parody of an Elizabethan sonnet, calling her piece "A Modern Sonnet to His Mistress's Eyebrows," in which the modern gallant in the lab observes her "noticeable winking of the eye at every beat" and then ungallantly simply adds the fact to his column of statistics.

Leon Solomons and Gertrude became fast friends; they liked working with each other and they enjoyed each other's company. Gertrude thought of him as her most intimate friend at Harvard and made him, along with her brother Leo and her adored Professor James, one of her triumvirate of cherished heroes. She particularly needed Solomons's companionship after her sophomore year when Leo was graduated and went off on a trip around the world. But nothing more came of their friendship. Solomons was called West to teach at Berkeley, and while they wrote to each other, now the whole continent separated them and the young scientist could no longer observe Gertrude's winking eyes or accelerating pulse at first hand. Solomons died while still a young man; some said of cancer, others reported an infection he picked up in his lab. Both William James and Gertrude mourned his untimely death.

On the whole, Gertrude's life at Radcliffe was a full, satisfying, intellectual adventure. Münsterberg, director of the psychology lab, called her his "ideal student." William James was delighted with her as a pupil and was eager to have her go on with her study of philosophy and psychology, which he always felt should be tied to the study of medicine. He thought that his own M.D. had been invaluable in his training. He was pleased when Gertrude decided she would go on as a graduate student to Johns Hopkins, which, unlike Harvard, was beginning to admit women to the school of medicine. Leo would be doing graduate work at Johns Hopkins, too; once more brother and sister could live together.

In her final exam in one of James's courses at Radcliffe, Gertrude—who had been up late the night before and the night before that, going to the opera in Boston instead of cramming for the exam—now looked around the big room where a score of earnest Radcliffe girls were plunging into answering the knotty philosophical questions. Gertrude looked the questions over and chewed on her pencil. "Keep an open mind," Professor James had always said. "Think for yourself."

Suddenly Gertrude began writing in her exam book. "Dear Prof. James," she wrote. "I am so sorry but really I do not feel like an examination paper in philosophy today." She signed it, took it up to the desk, and calmly walked out of the building into the fresh spring morning.

Next day the professor's reply came on a postcard: "Dear Miss Stein, I understand perfectly how you feel. I often feel like that myself."

Not everyone was so tolerant of Gertrude's cavalier attitude toward exams. In the spring of her senior year, 1897, she was reminded that until she passed the long-ignored college-entrance exam in Latin, she could not hope to graduate with her class.

Belatedly she began to study Latin declensions, but it was difficult to concentrate on them now that spring had once more filled the Cambridge air with the scent of lilacs. She took the exam and failed it. When she left college that June, although she had passed all her regular courses, she had to leave without her diploma. No matter. She was on her way West to visit brother Mike and his new wife Sarah in San Francisco. There would be time later in the summer to tackle that pesky Latin.

Gertrude knew that she would have to pass the exam in order to enroll in medical school in Baltimore and she wanted to do that—first, because Professor James wanted her to, then because Leo urged her to (Mike would send the necessary money), and because, well who could tell!, maybe if she had a brilliant career as a woman doctor and psychologist, that would be the way for her to make the name of Gertrude Stein famous!

A childhood photo of Gertrude Stein, taken in Paris COLLEC-
TION OF AMERICAN LITERATURE, BEINECKE LIBRARY, YALE
UNIVERSITY

Gertrude Stein (extreme left) *with her parents, brothers, and sister, in Vienna* COLLECTION OF AMERICAN LITERATURE, BEINECKE LIBRARY, YALE UNIVERSITY

Gertrude Stein (second from right) *during her college years*
COLLECTION OF AMERICAN LITERATURE, BEINECKE LIBRARY,
YALE UNIVERSITY

Gertrude Stein at the age of nineteen COLLECTION OF AMERI-
CAN LITERATURE, BEINECKE LIBRARY, YALE UNIVERSITY

Gertrude Stein in the Luxembourg Gardens, Paris, about 1905 THE BALTIMORE MUSEUM OF ART, CONE COLLECTION

Pablo Picasso's "Portrait of Leo Stein," 1906 THE BALTIMORE
MUSEUM OF ART, CONE COLLECTION

NINE

At first all went well. Gertrude studied under a tutor and concentrated on those mysterious Latin declensions long enough to pass that nagging Latin exam. Now she would get her Radcliffe diploma and be admitted to medical school.

In September 1897 she went back to Baltimore, this time settling happily into one of the city's row houses with Leo. Together they hung some of Leo's collection of Japanese prints to brighten the rather uninspiring walls. They employed a gentle woman servant to take care of their domestic needs. Now they were ready to enjoy months of each other's company, their relatives, new friendships, and to plunge into graduate-school studies with zeal—Leo already working in biology, Gertrude beginning medicine.

She encountered no male student so companionable as her brother was or so attractive as her Cambridge friend, Leon Solomons, had been. No new professor, not even the famous William Osler, captivated her dedicated devotion so much as had William James. Here what interested her most was finding herself one of a small select group of bright young women who were determined to brave the almost exclusively male world of medicine. They refused to be bothered by the men's condescending comments on their presence, the mildest of which was calling the women's dormitory "The Hen House." They refused to be baited by such juvenile questions as "Are you a doctor or a lady?" Gertrude and the others worked hard to prove themselves doctors—equal or more than equal to the men in their studies in the labs, lectures, and in surgery.

Most of Gertrude's new friends were honor students from Eastern women's colleges such as Bryn Mawr and Smith. As a Radcliffe graduate, Gertrude found she could hold her own with them intellectually in classes and could argue over the tea cups with the best of them. But they thought her a complete innocent in matters of sex, as indeed Gertrude herself recognized that she was. She was full of idealistic theories, however, and talked intensely about the importance of one's moral sense. She maintained that for her there were only two kinds of emotional involvement: on the one hand there was satisfying, affectionate comradeship, and on the other, complex physical passion, which she shrank from. It was not until her disastrous fourth year that Gertrude's attitudes toward sex were severely shaken by an unexpected emotional attachment to one of her fellow students.

But for the first three years she continued to enjoy pleasant and undisturbing comradeship with her classmates. In these three years she did well enough in her studies, though as time passed she began to realize that it was psychology rather than medicine that aroused her best efforts. The goal of becoming Gertrude Stein, M.D., began to have less and less appeal for her, especially after Leo, abandoning his studies in biology, left Baltimore to live and travel in Europe.

What Gertrude looked forward to then were her summer vacation trips, back to California to visit Mike and his artistic and vivacious wife Sarah and their small, curly-haired son Allan. Even more alluring were the summers she began to spend with the always entertaining Leo in Europe. He, having gone through a series of enthusiasms, was now immersed in an independent and serious study of aesthetics. No more formal university training for him! The museums and churches in Florence became his university, the masterpieces of quattrocentro art his studies.

Gertrude, visiting him, fell in love with Florence, enjoying with Leo his less serious pursuits in this handsome city of bridges, palazzos, and statues. She loved going with him on what they called "junking" trips, searching out on the Ponte Vecchio and in antique shops everywhere cast-off treasures such as old books, Renaissance furniture, Venetian glass, and even saints of wood or terra cotta. In Florence it was impossible not to become well acquainted with saints.

Under the hot Italian sun Gertrude enjoyed long walks up and down the hilly country roads lined with cypresses. Sometimes Leo went with her, sometimes a friend who had come over from Baltimore; often she went by herself. She liked talking with the voluble, friendly peasants she met on the dusty roads—unlike Leo, who sought out intellectuals such as Bernard Berenson, with whom he could discuss his latest analyses of the paintings of Piero della Francesca or Paolo Uccello. But Gertrude enjoyed these contacts too.

Most of all she and Leo enjoyed each other's company, gossiping about their friends, reminiscing about their childhood, arguing heatedly over books they were reading, paintings they were seeing, confiding in each other their ever changing ambitions. Leo disapproved of his sister's obviously waning interest in medicine. He admitted that he himself had lost interest in his study of history and now biology, but he pointed out that at least he had gone on to something else, something worthwhile. If Gertrude was growing halfhearted about becoming a doctor, what was she going to do instead? Gertrude did not know.

Because she did not know what else to do, she went back to Baltimore, resolving to finish her last year and get her degree. After all, that was what William James and Leo expected of her; and she did have friends there.

One of those who were pleased with her return was May Bookstaver, an attractive and bright young woman who was of the circle of friends who gathered at Mabel Haynes's place at teatime to discuss their lives and loves. May was one of those who admired Gertrude's mind but laughed indulgently at her naïveté in matters of sex.

One time May said it was obvious that Gertrude thought too much and felt too little. It showed in her fresh untouched face that she hadn't really lived, that she didn't even know how.

Gertrude was taken aback. Here she had prided herself on being an advanced student of human nature, but May and her friend Mabel and some of the others in the group thought her woefully immature. They asked whether she shrank from physical passion because of her moral sense or just because she lacked experience and was afraid.

In this and in more private discussions with May alone about sex, Gertrude too began to wonder if, after all, her high moral stand was a result not so much of conviction as of ignorance. Still, she staunchly maintained to May that physical passion should not be indulged in just for the sake of experience, of excitement. When May pointed out that passion could take many forms, Gertrude granted that passion might possibly be an acceptable part of an idealized relationship. Rather wistfully, she admitted to her that so far she had not

THEY NAMED ME GERTRUDE STEIN

experienced that kind of relationship. She wondered if she ever would.

May laughed. The two young women looked at each other intently, both quiet for a moment: Gertrude with her dark eyes open in wide appeal, May with her blue eyes filled with amusement. After a long silence between them Gertrude ventured to say that if she could find a good teacher, she thought she could be a good pupil, learning how meaningful a genuine emotional commitment could be.

May laughed again at Gertrude's artlessness. But this time her laugh could not disguise the fact that she was strongly drawn to Gertrude, with her keen mind, her sensitive face, appealing in its honesty and puzzled innocence. May knew that she would gladly undertake to be teacher to this wistful pupil. And Gertrude knew that she might be willing to be taught by this more experienced and sympathetic friend.

And so throughout the year, with a growing affection between these two, Gertrude was drawn into the realm of emotional involvement with one of her own sex. It wasn't easy for her; the relationship was fraught with doubts, with difficulties. Her first doubt was an old one, since she had always assumed that the only acceptable kind of deep attachment was that between a woman and a man. But here was a woman who was offering her more love and devotion than any man had ever shown her. Could that possibly be wrong?

Gertrude found herself responding hesitantly, at first with gratitude and then with growing eagerness. She wanted to believe completely in the genuineness of this new-found love which gave her periods of sheer happiness. But doubts and questions kept intruding. Was May perhaps just being teacher to a responsive pupil? Did she really care more for Gertrude than for anyone else, as she kept protesting she did? If so, why did May continue to spend so much time with her long-time friend Mabel, whose character and mind and spirit Gertrude thought distinctly inferior to May's and who was proving to be more and more annoyingly possessive? Gertrude could not bring herself to risk asking any questions about the relationship between those two. But she couldn't help wondering.

Her work at medical school, which had gone well her first three years, suffered badly in the last one. Now all her energies were spent in solving her own emotional problems. Psychiatry was the only subject that seemed relevant to her. Character—what people were really like, what she herself was like—this still seemed important. Other subjects, however, obstetrics particularly, proved to be a nightmare. The requirement that each fourth-year student deliver nine babies was one that she found distasteful and most difficult.

Gertrude, who had brought with her from Radcliffe a reputation for outstanding research, had become alienated, impatient with the whole concept of women in medicine. She flagrantly neglected all those subjects that did not interest her. As a result, she failed four of her courses. Her earnest classmates reproached her for her poor record, for letting down the cause of feminism. They did not understand what a crisis she was going through in her personal life. In the end, she did not get her degree. Gone were the early dreams of Gertrude Stein, future M.D. Would her present dreams of perfect emotional fulfillment disintegrate too? If her relationship with May was good and right, why did she so often alternate between happiness and despair? She felt she must get away to test herself, to figure things out.

She spent that summer in Tangiers and Granada, then

in Paris with Leo. Long letters from May reassured her. And when she read Dante's *Vita Nuova* she took hope and courage from the glimpses of pure love she found there.

On her return to the States and while spending a futile winter in Baltimore doing inconsequential research on the brain, she found herself involved once more in the apparently insoluble triangle. Mabel was not above using her unlimited money resources to bind May to her in obligation for gifts and for vacation trips. Why did May succumb to such a shameful connection? Perhaps she really wanted to break away as she said she did, but either she could not or she would not. Had she become hopelessly indebted to Mabel in some way?

Again Gertrude sailed for Europe to join Leo, to get a fresh perspective, determined to keep in touch with May only through occasional letters. Spring in Italy, summer in England, the fall in London—these were diverting but not healing. Gertrude spent hours in the British Museum, filling notebooks with passages from old English novels and with quotations that appealed to her. Each day she read until long after winter darkness shrouded all of London. Emerging at closing time, Gertrude found the smoky, grimy, foggy streets of London depressingly like the most dreary pages out of Dickens. Even Leo could not break her black mood and he left for livelier company in Paris.

In February, Gertrude herself fled from her loneliness and the gloom of London back to America. She lived for a while in New York with three cheerful, comradely woman friends, but really existed for her meetings with May in Baltimore. When these occurred, however, they proved unsatisfactory; nothing was changed, nothing solved. Her inner struggle continued between her love and admiration for May's better self and her revulsion at what she considered May's cowardly thralldom to Mabel.

In between these infrequent and unpredictable reunions, Gertrude turned in her frustration to writing. She began a novel about a family, her own family, the making of them as Americans. She also started another story, this one about three women caught in an emotional triangle. She wrote as she had written in her composition course at Radcliffe. This time she had no instructor to submit her writing to, but she felt she no longer needed one. Her style and even her spelling had greatly improved, although she wrote for herself alone.

In the early summer of 1903 she put away her barely begun manuscripts and joined Leo in Rome, not knowing when she would see May again. Then one day May and Mabel appeared together on the Via Nazionale. Was it by accident or design? Whichever it was, the situation became impossible as the three of them tried to keep up the hollow pretense of natural mutual friendliness. When they met again in Florence and Siena, the tension between the three of them grew unbearable. Mabel seemed now completely to have the upper hand. May had no shred of independence left.

That fall, Gertrude did not follow May back to the States. Instead, she settled in with Leo for an indefinite stay in Paris in his *pavillon* at 27, rue de Fleurus. She was American to the core, but she could not go home now.

After a period of brooding silence, she wrote one last letter to May, hoping to get her to see things as they were and to face up to a decisive solution to their dilemma. May's answer was just one more of her loving but evasive and ambiguous statements of how things might be better between them in the future. At last Gertrude admitted to herself that May would never be strong enough to act decisively. It was up to Gertrude to make the break. It was one of the hardest things she ever had to do, but she stopped all communication with May. No more letters, no more meetings. It was over!

Now Gertrude re-read all the old letters that had passed between them—copies of hers that she had kept, May's letters that she had saved. She re-read them in order to see the entire experience as a whole and to re-shape and finish the manuscript she had begun in New York. In her story she changed the names of the three young women involved, calling herself Adele, but she changed none of the facts. She traced the whole affair from its innocent beginnings through its joyful and pain-ful ups and downs, on through to its sorry conclusion. As always, it was character that interested her, her own most of all. She wrote in a forthright, straightforward way, neither in self-pity nor in self-blame, but clearly seeing things, seeing herself and the other two as they were. When she finished it she called her story "Q.E.D." and hid it away. She hoped she had proved something to herself. It was still too personal and too painful an ac-count to show to anyone. Only Leo knew something of what she had been doing as she spent long hours in solitude bent over her desk.

Now she turned back to Leo and his interests, hoping to be drawn out of her misery, longing to regain some of her old serenity and eventually even some of her care-free joy in living.

But one good thing she had discovered and that was that writing itself could be the most gratifying, the most satisfying, the most absorbing activity of all. She would go on writing, perhaps some day resuming the long story of her own family. Meanwhile, there was Leo. She needed him; they needed each other.

TEN

As Gertrude Stein wrote many years later, "Paris, France was peaceful and exciting."

In 1903, when she moved into Leo's apartment at 27, rue de Fleurus, it seemed at first more peaceful than exciting. She was glad of that. She felt at home in Paris, remembering a happy year there when she was three and four years old, waiting there with her mother and brothers for their father to complete long business trips.

She remembered attending a small school with French children, having soup and thick bread for breakfast, at lunch trading her mutton for spinach that another little girl wanted to get rid of. Imagine liking mutton better than spinach! She remembered joyfully swinging on the low swags of chains that looped around the Arc de Triomphe. When she entered a shop even now and sniffed, she could remember just how her mother's French perfumes and gloves smelled and the small sealskin muff that her mother had bought her long ago, for the same delightful smells of perfume and leather and fur were still in the air a quarter of a century later.

So here she was again, feeling at home but conscious that she had changed almost more than Paris had. Now she was twenty-nine years old. With mixed feelings she saw in the mirror that her face had subtly changed in just the past year. It was more thoughtful, even stronger, and to one who looked closely there were signs of strain, even suffering. She decided ruefully that no one could accuse her now of looking "unlived and youthful" as she used to or of being so innocently content with herself and her old naïve ambitions.

Worn by her recent emotional struggles, and finding some release in writing, she welcomed the quiet pleasures of living in Leo's new home, which was back from the street, tucked away on the far side of a courtyard. The familiar Japanese prints covered the walls of the big studio-living room, which was separated by a few short steps from the building that contained their dining and sleeping rooms. Leo had also hung the one painting he had bought in England just to prove to himself that he didn't have to be a millionaire to own an oil.

Gertrude helped her brother rearrange the heavily carved furniture that she liked and that he had acquired in Italy, and the various treasures they both had picked up on their many "junking trips." She even enjoyed unpacking her cheap souvenirs of Florence that she had a weakness for—such as the miniature alabaster bird-baths or the urns with the inevitable pair of marble birds perched on their rims. She liked them and didn't care whether anyone else did or not.

For the time being, Gertrude was content with peaceful family life. Mike and Sarah had come to Paris and were living nearby in rue Madame. Gertrude saw much of them and enjoyed taking her young nephew on his Thursdays off from school to the Luxembourg Gardens, that children's paradise of bouncing balls, rolling hoops, and toy sailing boats.

Best of all, there was Leo, Leo who was obviously glad to have his sister again as companion and audience. If for a while Gertrude talked less volubly, laughed less heartily, and argued less vehemently with her brother than she used to, at least she listened to him with much of her old admiring attention.

Leo, too, looked older. He was growing to look and sound more and more like an earnest professor. His gold-rimmed spectacles, his high intellectual forehead topped by his gleaming bald head, his long nose drooping over his red-gold moustache—all this tended to make him a rather formidable figure to everyone except Gertrude. She liked the way his tall thin body fell into oddly graceful poses, making him look at times like a long-legged heron about to take flight. She liked his enthusiasms in art, one of which was his recent attempt to become a painter himself.

That happened quite suddenly the year before. One night while expounding his theories of art with a young musician friend, Pablo Casals, Leo felt an overwhelming urge to try his own hand at painting. Hurrying back to his chilly hotel room, he lighted a fire in the stove, took off his clothes, stood before the full-length mirror of his *armoire,* and began to draw. For weeks afterward he haunted the Louvre, drawing feverishly from the statues there. He even enrolled at the Académie Julian, seeking professional models and instruction. After he moved to quarters on rue de Fleurus with its separate studio, and by the time Gertrude had joined him there, his zeal for becoming a working artist was fading. Again, his long habit of theorizing took over and he spent more time in analyzing his work than in actually covering canvas.

Perhaps, he decided, if he couldn't be a great painter, he might become a collector. He knew he could not afford old masterpieces; so he prowled through the galleries and shops of Paris, looking for new art that would

THEY NAMED ME GERTRUDE STEIN

excite or please him as much as had the quattrocento paintings he had studied in Florence.

Finally, in order to prove to the dealers that he wasn't just wasting his time and theirs, he bought and paid for a pleasant painting by Du Gardier of a woman in white with a white dog on a green lawn. But once hung on his studio walls, the picture neither excited nor satisfied him. Leo longed for an adventure. He felt ready to make a daring leap into the world of twentieth-century art. But, as he told Gertrude, nothing that he saw tempted him to jump.

Finally Bernard Berenson, himself a man of the Renaissance, was the one who gave him the necessary push. "Cézanne!" B.B. said. "Cézanne's paintings are the ones you should see"—and directed him to the dealer Vollard, on rue Laffitte.

When Leo went to Ambroise Vollard's shop he succumbed at once to the new geometrics of Cézanne's paintings. Here was what he had been looking for all along. Cézanne was no insubstantial shimmering impressionist. Into his solid work had gone all the reasoned effort, the logical construction, the controlled skill that Leo admired and sought in his own life. Obviously Cézanne, too, put thinking before feeling, without abandoning a deep personal love of nature and of the countryside around his home in Aix-en-Provence. Cézanne, Leo learned, was not young. But he was new to Leo and just what Leo wanted. Promptly he bought "Landscape with Springhouse," and carried it home in triumph. Down came several Japanese prints to make way for the new treasure.

Gertrude caught some of Leo's enthusiasm for Cézanne. On holiday in Florence the next summer she went with him, not to the Uffizi galleries, which he had formerly haunted, but to Charles Loeser's villa to see the Cézannes that Bernard Berenson said were hidden away there. Loeser was an American, a Harvard friend of B.B.'s who had abandoned the family department store in Brooklyn to become an art critic and live in Florence. Gertrude and Leo saw in the formal salons of his villa perfect pieces of quattrocento art. But when they were admitted to the private bedrooms and dressing rooms they gasped at the sight of the many Cézannes that Loeser owned and had hung there for his own enjoyment.

It was a happy summer for Leo. He spent many hours at Loeser's studying the Cézanne paintings with as much intensity as the artist himself had shown in studying his models and his landscapes, and the still lifes, too, with their apples, their linen tablecloths that fell into crumpled folds on the table.

Gertrude's study of Cézanne was more intuitive, much less concentrated. In the end she preferred being out-of-doors, walking through real landscapes under the hot Italian sun, munching ripe fruit that fell from real trees, and dining with Leo from smooth tablecloths in their rented villa in Fiesole high in the hills above Florence.

Sometimes the brother and sister would together take the long hot walk to Berenson's cool villa, I Tatti, where there were Renaissance paintings on the walls, always good lively talk about art, which pleased Leo, a fine library that pleased Gertrude, and delightful hospitality with delicious luncheons and teas that pleased everyone.

The Steins looked quite different from their host. Berenson was small, delicate, elegant, and meticulous in his unending search for beauty in every aspect of his life. Tall, gangling Leo thought Berenson's ego too apparent but justified, and found his mind fascinating. Gertrude, in B.B.'s slight, compact presence, may have

THEY NAMED ME GERTRUDE STEIN

felt at first bigger, heavier, and more cumbersome than usual. But she showed no self-consciousness as she calmly emptied her sandals of gravel at the entrance to the villa, slapped the road dust from her voluminous corduroy garment, or tugged the cloth free from the places where it stuck to her perspiring body.

Because of their passion for books, the Steins were always given the run of the magnificent Berenson library. It bothered their host, however, when both Leo and Gertrude would stretch out full length on the cool library floor, cigars or tall glasses of lemonade perilously in hand, while they turned pages of precious manuscripts or expensively illustrated art histories. Rare editions meant little to Gertrude, whose chief interest was what a book said, not what its binding was or what date it bore.

Leo was undoubtedly better than his sister at a favorite art game the Berensons sometimes played with guests after dinner. Everyone gathered around a table that had many photographs of paintings scattered over it. Someone would choose a painting at random and cover it with paper through which a small hole had been cut. Now only an unexpected detail of the painting could be seen: a hand, a halo, a fold in a cloak, part of a face. From that small glimpse of the work, its treatment, its "tactile value," people were to guess who the artist was.

Berenson, the authority, almost always knew; it was both his profession and his joy to study and recognize the brushstrokes of the masters. Leo often knew, especially if it was quattrocento art. Other guests occasionally recognized what they were looking at, for everyone in Florence talked art endlessly. Gertrude seldom knew, but her hearty laugh at her own ignorance was so disarming that no one could hold it against her. Mabel Dodge, another frequent guest, thought the best thing about these parties was Gertrude's laugh. It was full-bodied, nourishing, completely satisfying. "It's like beef-steak," she said.

And indeed Gertrude's laugh rang out more and more frequently as she put her unhappiness further behind her. Back in Paris, she found the city still peaceful but growing more exciting all the time.

ELEVEN

Gertrude and Leo were becoming well-known figures on the streets of Paris. No one could forget *les Américains* striding side by side down the boulevards or walking one behind the other in the narrow streets like the rue Cassette. Both the tall lean brother and the shorter, heavy sister wore brown corduroys and sandals that turned up at the toes—"like the prows of gondolas," someone said. Leo was beginning to grow a beard that gave promise of becoming handsome. Gertrude's lustrous brown hair was coiled on top of her head like a small, heavy, but very secure crown.

One day soon after their return from Florence they were making their way with some excitement to Vollard's. A Cézanne, that's what they were after. Gertrude now was as eager as Leo to have another Cézanne for their own walls. Vollard was a gloomy man; his shop was a cluttered place. He greeted the two Americans in his usual suspicious manner but thawed out a little when they said Loeser had sent them. They wanted to see some landscapes by Cézanne. None was in view. Vollard disappeared. Gertrude and Leo heard him climbing steps. There was a long wait; then Vollard came down with a small painting of an apple. It was a fine apple, a typical Cézanne apple, but not what they had in mind just now. A landscape perhaps?

Again Vollard climbed steps and again he reappeared

with a painting, this time of a nude back. Lovely, yes, but what about a landscape instead? Vollard again disappeared, coming back from upstairs with a large canvas, one small part of it containing an unfinished landscape. Yes, that was more like it. But—and Gertrude and Leo exchanged despairing glances—what they really wanted was one of those sunny, red-roofed landscapes painted with all the artist's magnificent strength and love of his land near Aix. The kind they had seen at Loeser's—a large one, a finished one.

Vollard nodded and disappeared once again. It was growing late. Leo and Gertrude were discouraged. Down the stairs came slow footsteps but this time it was not Vollard, just an old charwoman on her way home. Soon another charwoman descended, mumbled to them, and went out the door.

Suddenly Gertrude started to laugh. She rocked back and forth in glee. "You see," she gasped, "Vollard has no Cézannes! He doesn't understand what we want, so he goes upstairs, tells the charwomen to paint something for those crazy Americans, and that's why he brings us these unfinished canvases!" Gertrude whooped with delight at her invention, and Leo joined in, shaking with laughter at the joke.

When Vollard finally reappeared, they quickly controlled themselves because this time he held in his hands a Cézanne landscape. It was one of marvelous green. Both Leo and Gertrude fell in love with it, promptly bought it, and hurried home in the dusk with their new treasure.

Much of the excitement of that winter of 1905 in Paris was in buying new paintings for their studio room—small ones usually, Cézanne nudes, a black and white Manet, and two small Renoirs. Later they bought two

THEY NAMED ME GERTRUDE STEIN

Gauguins, "rather awful," Gertrude said at first, but she grew to like them.

And then, as the grand climax, Gertrude and Leo persuaded Mike that they just had to have money for a large Cézanne portrait. They promised that after that they would indulge in no more extravagance for that year. As always, Mike gave in to their eager pleas. He and Sarah were more sympathetic now because they also were beginning to collect paintings. After much pondering, Leo and Gertrude decided upon a portrait of a woman, a portrait of Mme Cézanne seated in a red chair. It was important to Leo as a crowning addition to his growing art collection, a painting that he could expound upon to friends who came to see the new art.

But it was even more important to Gertrude because it was under the stimulus of this portrait that she began writing again. In February she began to write what she at first called *Three Histories*, later named *Three Lives*. Now Paris was both exciting and peaceful to her, for the very act of writing was to her at once peaceful and exciting.

Leo neither encouraged nor discouraged her. If it seemed to him that she spent too much time alone scribbling, that was her privilege. And if in her turn she sometimes found it difficult to give her full attention to another one of Leo's analytical and repetitious monologues on their paintings, she sat quietly while friends and even a few strangers kept coming to 27, rue de Fleurus on Saturday nights just to look and to listen. If in their diverging interests the brother and sister were beginning ever so slightly to drift apart, neither one was yet aware of it.

Gertrude was absorbed in her writing. She had been reading and translating the French writer Flaubert, whose character Félicité in *Un Coeur Simple* was a servant woman who reminded her of the various servants with simple hearts she had known in Baltimore. But she felt even more the influence of Cézanne as a portrait painter. Cézanne was obviously interested in character; so was she. Every part of his portrait of a woman was as important as every other part. He gave equal attention to every small detail of his composition. That was what Gertrude wanted to do in her writing.

And so, sitting at the long carved table beneath the Cézanne portrait, looking up at it from time to time, Gertrude started to write her own studies of women, to describe three lives. "The Good Anna" was first. Here she wrote of a German immigrant housekeeper—a type she had known in Baltimore. "The Gentle Lena" was written next—another simple type, kind and good, based on the servant she and Leo had in their Baltimore days. And finally, "Melanctha," a black woman—more complicated, more impetuous, whose character Gertrude showed in a series of psychological confrontations with her lover and with another woman. Here Gertrude's recollections of blacks in Baltimore, crowding into her mind, were shaped and set down on paper. The three women of her stories had not known each other, but Gertrude had known each of them or their types—how they thought and felt and talked. This was important, for it was through their repetitious talk that Gertrude showed the beginning of a style that was to become uniquely her own: revealing character by insistent repetition, each repetition with only the slightest significant variation.

Would anyone ever read her writings? She did not know and at the moment did not care, although she was disappointed that Leo was not much impressed. But to Flaubert and Cézanne, Gertrude was grateful. The writing of the one and the painting of the other had got her going again.

She kept writing slowly and steadily but was willing to break off at times for long walks or to go to art galleries with Leo and to attend exhibitions with the family group.

When in the fall of that same year, 1905, the four Steins—Gertrude and Leo, Michael and Sarah—walked into the Salon d'Automne in the Petit Palais on opening day, they went with a good deal of eager excitement, for Paris was full of rumors about how wild and different some of the paintings were. This was the first time that an official Salon was ever held in the autumn, so that rebellious and independent painters who had not been admitted to the Salon in the spring in the Grand Palais would have a chance to be seen all together by the curious public. In the first few rooms the Steins saw nothing revolutionary. Soon, though, from a room farther on, they heard an angry buzzing as though a beehive had been upset and the bees were angrily swarming around, attacking an intruder.

The angry buzzing became a low roaring from a crowd in Room VII, where the Steins discovered the walls covered with paintings of such violent color they almost shouted for attention. No wonder these artists were called *les fauves*, or "wild beasts," by a critic who saw that, by the clamorous color of their paintings and the uproar they caused, they quite overwhelmed a conventional statue of a cupid that stood lost and neglected in the center of the room.

Most vociferous were the people gathered around a painting called *La Femme au Chapeau*, or "Woman with the Hat," by Henri Matisse. They were mocking it, half angry, half joking, as they pointed out to each other the green stripe across the woman's forehead and down her long nose, the vermilion eyebrows, the one cheek which was pinkish red, the other a yellowish green. The hat piled high with artificial fruit was striking in its greens, blues, and purples, and the woman's green-gloved hand was holding a large fan that covered her bosom.

The four Steins stared in amazement at the painting. Leo's immediate reaction was to say that it was the nastiest smear of paint he had ever seen. But as he looked, his amazement changed to admiration. All those colors, bold and unexpected as they were, added up to a true and stunning portrait. Why was the crowd so upset by it? Why was one young man so indignant that he threatened to scratch off the thick pigment with his own hands? Leo and Gertrude, Mike and Sarah recognized that the portrait was indeed done in a bold new style, something so extraordinary that it bowled everyone over. But the longer the Steins looked at it, the more exhilarated they became. Gertrude even began to think that after all it looked perfectly natural. Sarah called it superb. Almost simultaneously the four of them concluded that they must have it in the family.

Leo, still their leader in affairs of art, took Gertrude with him into the secretary's office to ask the price. The portrait was listed at 500 francs. Because they were told that an artist seldom expected the asking price, Leo and Gertrude offered 400 francs, sending word through the secretary to Matisse, who had been so upset by the hostile reaction of the public to this portrait of his wife that he had left the exhibition, vowing not to return.

Gertrude and Leo, coming back the next day, learned that Matisse had turned down their offer. The painting was for sale at 500 francs or $100—no less. Did the Americans still want it? Again they looked long at the daring portrait. Again they felt the tremendous power of the painting. Again they were upset at the jeers of the crowd. It did not take them long to agree to the 500 francs. At the end of the exhibition they went home jubilant over their prize.

"Woman with the Hat," the sensation of the show, was now the sensation at 27, rue de Fleurus.

TWELVE

The portrait that was to play the biggest part in Gertrude's life was a portrait of herself painted by a young, almost unknown Spanish artist, Pablo Picasso.

It was Leo who discovered the work of Picasso in Paris, but it was Gertrude who discovered the young man himself. Leo came home one day with a painting of Picasso's, "The Acrobat's Family with a Monkey." The ape was looking at the child as lovingly as the parents were. This made the dealer, an ex-clown named Sagot, say that Picasso must have painted the whole group from life. Leo said no real ape looked at an infant that way. Nevertheless, he liked the grouping and the entire painting so much that he bought it and took Gertrude back to Sagot's with him to see more of the young Spaniard's work.

An awkwardly tender young nude, posed for by a girl named Linda who sometimes sold flowers outside the Moulin Rouge, caught Leo's fancy on this next visit. But Gertrude did not at first like the painting at all. "Her legs and feet are drawn like a monkey's; they are repulsive," she protested. She argued vehemently with Leo about it in front of Sagot, the dealer. Anxious to please the Americans and eager to sell the painting, Sagot suggested a simple solution. "If you do not like the legs and feet, let us guillotine her; we can cut off the lower half so that you can take her home without the legs and feet." And indeed Gertrude did like the head of the girl and the basket of red flowers she was holding in her thin arms against her thin chest. But of course it would be sacrilege to mutilate an artist's work in that way, in any way. Both Leo and Gertrude promptly refused to have the canvas cut.

At dinner the next night Leo announced that he had gone back and bought "Young Girl with a Basket of Flowers." Gertrude threw down her napkin. "You knew I hated it," she said angrily.

But all that changed when Gertrude met the young artist in person. Pablo Picasso was seven years younger than Gertrude, dark, Spanish, with a lock of thick black hair that fell down over his forehead but not over his bottomless dark eyes that seemed to absorb everything.

To Picasso, Gertrude was an astonishing new type— vital, expansive, with a noble head, a ready laugh, and the frankness of a completely unselfconscious American. The two took to each other at once. When Picasso asked if he might paint her portrait, Gertrude was pleased and her answer was a prompt yes.

Picasso and Fernande Bellevallée, the beautiful young woman who was living with him, were invited to 27, rue de Fleurus for dinner the next Saturday night. Any formality was completely shattered when Gertrude, in the midst of conversation, absently picked up a piece of bread near her plate. "That's mine," said the hungry Picasso indignantly, snatching it from her hand. Then he looked so abashed at what he had done that Gertrude burst out laughing with that laugh of hers as smooth and rich as the Chantilly cream they were going to have with dessert.

Gertrude found Picasso's studio in a ramshackle old tenement building near the top of Montmartre on rue Ravignan. The rickety building looked something like the big square laundry barges that were tied up in the river Seine, so the artists and writers who lived there nicknamed the place *Bateau Lavoir*. The long narrow hallways were like passageways on a boat. The *lavoir* part of the name was given in mockery because in the whole establishment there was only one faucet with running water for washing or cooking. This was shared by Picasso and the dozen or so other poor young artists and writers who lived in a bewildering maze of shabby rooms on several floors. Picasso's studio, like all the others, was without gas or electricity. But the rent was cheap and that was important to all the inhabitants, whose ambitions were much larger than their incomes.

On her first visit, Gertrude was startled by the incredibly messy confusion of Picasso's place. Off at one end of the studio she could see a tiny adjoining room that Picasso called the bedroom because it was almost filled by an old couch. But the couch was so covered by portfolios spilling over with unfinished drawings that Gertrude wondered how anyone could sleep there. In the studio itself, a small stove in one corner obviously did for both cooking and heating. Gertrude hoped that the cooking was more satisfactory than the heating, which she could scarcely feel in this cold and drafty room. The winter light that filtered in through blue windows was pale and bleak. Chairs here and there might have made the place more comfortable, except that they were piled so high with papers or odds and ends of clothing that no one could sit down on them. A contented-looking mongrel dog was tied to the leg of one rickety chair. Gertrude, always attracted to dogs, hesitated to pat Frika for fear she had fleas. The only piece of furniture that might once have been rather elegant was a scarred table used for meals when it wasn't being used for a washstand; pitchers and basins and dishes were jumbled together

THEY NAMED ME GERTRUDE STEIN

along with tin cans holding paintbrushes. The brushes and the easels gave a clue to the main purpose of the room—it was an artist's workshop. Large canvases leaned against the walls—paintings of clowns or acrobats mostly, a few nudes. Sketches and drawings littered the floor.

Before Gertrude could take it all in, a large broken-down chair was miraculously cleared of its clutter for her to make herself comfortable in. Picasso sat on a small straight kitchen chair, pulled it up close to his easel, mixed brown and gray on his small palette, and went to work.

Gertrude's pose was a natural one for her. She sat alert but at ease, her slender hands resting lightly on her knees, which were held slightly apart. Her heavy clothes wrapped her bulk almost completely in dark brown, allowing only the white ruffles of her blouse to show. These were held together at her throat by a handsome coral brooch. The pin glowed, Gertrude's face glowed.

The beautiful Fernande came in and out, read aloud one or two of La Fontaine's stories in her mellifluous voice to entertain Gertrude. She made tea for them all on the small stove during the rest periods.

But it was Picasso's vital presence that filled and warmed the room for Gertrude. It was the intensity of the look he fixed upon her and the concentration of his dark gaze that made her feel that he was dredging up her innermost thoughts and discovering her basic nature—even as she herself was always trying to do with others. The difference was that she put her discoveries down on paper; Picasso put his on canvas.

When in the late afternoon Leo and Michael and Sarah arrived to see what progress the young artist was making, they were so impressed by his preliminary sketch in oils that they urged him to let it stand as it was.

But Picasso was firm. Even if the Steins were satisfied with what he had done, he himself was not. There was still a long way to go before he would call it a portrait.

And so the sittings continued throughout the winter. In those months Gertrude kept writing, finishing the story of the black Melanctha. For her the sittings were not an interruption of her writing; they were a reinforcement of it, of her moods, of her insight into her character's identity. Picasso and Paris might seem a world away from Melanctha and Baltimore. But to Gertrude the long walks or her long rides on the horse-drawn omnibus across the city and up to Picasso's studio, her long talks with the artist during what turned out to be eighty or ninety sittings, the long solitary walks back home in the early winter dusk—all these stimulated her writing. They helped her form those increasingly long sentences as they slowly unwound in her mind to be put down on paper later at night.

Nighttime was the best time to write, Gertrude found. Too many evening hours were interrupted by callers curious to see the constantly growing Stein collection of paintings that was becoming famous throughout Paris. Finally, in self-defense, Leo and Gertrude settled on Saturday nights for having "open house," so that even strangers would know they were welcome that one night in the week.

Usually Leo eagerly lectured to the visitors on the meaning of the new art, even when the callers were young artists themselves brought to the hospitable Americans' place by Matisse or Picasso. It was up to Gertrude to help entertain the visitors, although her role seemed often to be chiefly to see to it that their excellent cook, Hélène, put out a tempting spread of hams, cheeses, and long loaves of freshly baked bread.

Often Gertrude stayed in the background, watching

THEY NAMED ME GERTRUDE STEIN

the visitors with intense interest, trying to figure out their types. When Picasso came, frequently for dinner on Saturday nights, it was Gertrude who gave him special welcome, and later in the studio she would even rescue him occasionally from Leo's too insistent lectures on his vast collection of Japanese prints.

When spring came to Paris, when the chestnut trees in the Luxembourg Gardens were lighted like chandeliers with bright blossoms, and when everyone started making plans for the great summer exodus, Gertrude's sittings for Picasso came to an end. The Steins were going to Florence, Picasso was going to Spain. Gertrude had finished "Melanctha." Although everyone thought that Picasso had finished his stunning portrait of Gertrude, suddenly one day he wiped out the whole head with turpentine. "I cannot see you any more when I look," he said in frustration. Off he went to Spain, leaving the unfinished canvas up against the wall in the *Bateau Lavoir*. There it stayed all summer, Gertrude with her brown robe, white ruffle, coral brooch, hands on knees—and no head! Gertrude had not allowed "Young Girl with a Basket of Flowers" to be guillotined but she could not prevent Picasso from using the guillotine on her own portrait.

THIRTEEN

The moment Pablo Picasso came back from Spain in the fall, he took up his brushes and painted in Gertrude's head before he even saw her. On canvas her face became a mask like the pre-Roman Iberian masks Picasso had discovered. Her eyes were almond-shaped, one larger than the other; one side of her face thrust forward, the other receded, while the mouth was a curving line, joining the two together. Suddenly in the painting Gertrude's face had become strong—not so much what Picasso had seen but what he knew. From now on, his paintings would be different from any he had done before.

When they first looked at the new portrait, people were astonished. "But Mlle Gertrude does not look like that," they protested. Picasso answered confidently, "She will." The artist and his subject were the only ones who really liked the portrait. Many years later Gertrude said, "I was and I still am satisfied with my portrait, for me, it is I, and it is the only reproduction of me which is always I, for me."

A gift from the artist, the portrait was hung by Leo under Gertrude's direction in a prominent place on the crowded walls of the studio at 27, rue de Fleurus.

Before Picasso finished his portrait, Gertrude had finished *Three Lives*, but more and more she herself was living two lives—an outer life and an inner one. Outwardly she followed the busy, gossipy round of exciting artistic events with Leo and with friends.

In the summer, she went with Leo to Florence or Fiesole, where they rented a villa. There she went often to lunch with the Berensons, who always had a houseful of interesting guests and gorgeous gardens to explore. She enjoyed long walks under the intense Italian sun.

In winter, she found herself with Leo receiving more and more people on their Saturday nights at home in their studio. She continued to have long talks with Picasso, not so often now with Leo. Leo was growing deaf and was less inclined to listen to others, more and more inclined to do most of the talking himself. All four of the Steins called on the Matisses from time to time in their high apartment with its view of Notre Dame and the Seine. In contrast to the Picasso dwelling, the Matisse place was scrupulously neat and clean. Even so, while Sarah preferred Matisse, his paintings and his background, Gertrude felt more at home with Picasso even in the chaos he shared with Fernande. She still enjoyed her long solitary walks under the wintry sun or the rainy skies of Paris.

But all this time Gertrude was becoming more and more absorbed in an inner life, in her writing. She wrote in pencil on loose pages or in a French school child's notebook—none of which made a properly prepared manuscript to send off to a publisher. When she confessed that trying to type made her nervous, a good friend from Baltimore, Miss Etta Cone, generously offered to type *Three Lives* for her.

Through another friend in New York the typed stories were submitted to an editor, Pitts Duffield, who rejected them, writing, "The book is too unconventional for one thing, and if I may say so, too literary."

The stories were then passed on to an agent in New York, and he was pessimistic about selling them, saying, "They seem to me to be more character sketches than anything else."

Gertrude was discouraged but also indignant. What was wrong with stories being unconventional, literary, and full of character! That is just what she had meant them to be.

Very few people seemed to grasp what she was trying to do. When Gertrude showed her manuscript to Mike's wife, Sarah was moved by her writing, although she did not completely understand it. Her warm response touched Gertrude. Leo, though, had nothing to say about her work and gave her no encouragement whatever. His silent disapproval hurt her more than she cared to acknowledge. If Leo, her own brother, deserted her, whom could she count on?

She would count on herself, that's what she would do! So when Gertrude seriously undertook the long long task of writing *Making of Americans,* she immersed herself in it, in hours of solitude, with no hope that anyone except herself, or perhaps a stranger sometime, somewhere, would ever read or understand what she was trying to say. This new book was to be even more revolutionary in style than *Three Lives,* different from anything she had ever written; different even from anything she had ever read. Its method, Gertrude thought with satisfaction, was as new as the twentieth century itself!

This book that started out as a history of Gertrude's own family—her grandparents, who had come from the Old World; their descendants making their way in America, the New World—gradually became her much larger attempt at writing a history of all types of people everywhere. But in the writing she did not make it a

THEY NAMED ME GERTRUDE STEIN

narrative with a beginning, a middle, and an end but let it become a slow-moving, slowly advancing stream of consciousness and, as she said, "a groping for a continuous present, a beginning again and again." Sometimes she grew discouraged, afraid that the ordinary reader might very well be lost in the maze of sentences that could seem every bit as puzzling as the twisting corridors and the many levels of the *Bateau Lavoir*. But Gertrude was sure that on persisting, a sympathetic reader could find the way with as much ease as she herself did. Would she ever find such a reader? Unexpectedly she did.

For years Gertrude had kept diagrams and charts of characters that she wanted to analyze and present in her writing. One way in which she explored other personalities was to read their letters when she could, even those of people she did not know. An American friend in Paris, for instance, let Gertrude read letters from one of her friends in California—an Alice B. Toklas, two or three years younger than Gertrude, whom she had never met, although Mike and Sarah knew her "back home."

Alice's letters showed her to be an unusual young woman—the letters were witty, whimsical, perceptive, and while conventional, they revealed an unexpected streak of tolerance for the unconventional in others. By the time Alice Toklas came to Paris in 1907 and Gertrude saw her, she felt that she already knew her well and would like to know her better.

When, the year before, Alice Toklas had seen in San Francisco the astonishing paintings by Matisse brought there by the Michael Steins on a visit home, and when she heard some of Sarah's stories of life in Paris with Gertrude and Leo, she made up her mind to go see this brave new art world for herself. "Just for a visit," she told her widowed father. She traveled with a young woman friend, Harriet Levy, a California neighbor and writer.

On their first day in Paris the two went to call on the Michael Steins. There for the first time Gertrude and Alice met face to face. Gertrude thought the newcomer attractive; Alice was small and slender; she had dark eyes that sparkled, dark hair that shone, a gypsy-like air about her with her long swinging earrings and exotic, brightly colored dress. She looked unsophisticated and at the same time wise, at once both trusting and shrewd. Gertrude took to her right away.

On her part Alice was overwhelmed by Miss Stein, her large golden-brown presence, the sense she gave off of abundant life. Alice admired the coral brooch she wore and her deep velvety voice, especially her laugh that seemed to Alice to start from deep down and somehow emerge through that brooch at her throat. Later Alice was to say that whenever she met a genius, a bell within her rang. Upon meeting Gertrude Stein, she distinctly heard the bell pealing loud and clear.

Gertrude, wanting to see more of Alice, offered to take her the next day on one of her favorite walks—through the Luxembourg Gardens. Alice looked pleased at being singled out in this way and agreed to come to Miss Stein's apartment first so they could set out together. At two o'clock, then?

All the next morning Gertrude found herself looking forward eagerly to her engagement with this stranger who was not really a stranger and who gave promise of being a real friend. It was something of a blow, then, to receive toward noon by *petit bleu* the message that since Alice and Harriet Levy had decided to have lunch together in the Bois, Alice might be somewhat delayed, but she would come as soon after lunch as possible.

Gertrude was taken aback. At first she was disappointed, then annoyed, and finally upset. What if her guest did not come at all? By the time Alice Toklas did appear and was admitted into the studio, it was quite late, and Gertrude, angry by now, made no attempt to hide the fact. Pacing back and forth behind the long Renaissance table like a wrathful goddess, she let her visitor know at once that she expected her guests to be prompt. She was not used to being put off in this way. She quoted Picasso as always saying that punctuality was the courtesy of kings. She made it clear that she expected that same courtesy from her guests, certainly from one whom she had chosen as companion to share in her favorite pastime, taking a walk in the Luxembourg. If Miss Toklas had any notion of their seeing much of each other in the future, certain matters such as promptness must be understood from the start. Was that clear?

Alice, obviously dumfounded at this attack and at the changed, unsmiling countenance of her new friend, could only nod in agreement as Gertrude continued to rebuke her.

Then, as though suddenly aware of Alice's innocent and stricken look, Gertrude was silent, her face softened. She was no longer the wrathful goddess. She became instead the welcoming friend, the hospitable hostess.

"It is not too late to go for a walk," she said, smiling. "You can look at the pictures while I change my clothes."

Did Gertrude admit to herself that her anger must have been due to fear—fear that Alice had been deliberately putting her off, putting her in second place? Fear that this new friendship that Gertrude was counting on so much would not live up to her expectations unless from the very beginning she took the stand that all must be honest and forthright and clearly understood between them. Gertrude remembered too well the distrust, the ambiguities, the evasions of that long-ago friendship with May—a friendship that had ended in an unhappy stalemate. Gertrude would not want to risk another such debacle! This time she would make sure of undivided loyalty. In return, she herself was ready and eager to give total loyalty if this new friendship developed as she hoped.

That afternoon in the Luxembourg Gardens, Gertrude took pleasure in entertaining her guest. She took her along her favorite walks, giving all the while lively accounts of the history of these Renaissance gardens with their marble fountains, double staircases, stone balustrades. She was amusing about the various statues flanking the octagonal basin—Venus leaving the bath and David conquering Goliath. She knew the names of various aromatic herbs that made up the handsome low hedges that bordered the walks. When she discovered that her companion was interested in the espaliered fruit trees that they saw in one corner of the gardens, she drew her out on the kinds of orchards they had both known as children back in California. Gertrude was a most delightful guide. And as a sign that she had completely forgiven the younger woman for her heedless tardiness Gertrude addressed her by her first name. Ignoring accepted convention on such short acquaintance, she called her "Alice." In her turn, Alice was pleased by this friendly overture; by now she was completely charmed by this bright and outgoing personality. But she continued that day to address her new friend as "Miss Stein." And so the pattern was set. For the time being, at least, Miss Gertrude Stein was the leader, Alice B. Toklas the follower.

Slowly and certainly over the next years there developed between them the closest and most lasting friendship that either woman had ever known.

FOURTEEN

As Gertrude's friendship with Alice deepened, it mattered less and less to her that Leo expressed no interest in his sister's odd and innovative writing.

Alice read the manuscript of *Three Lives* and, after the first shock of strangeness wore off, not only appreciated it and praised it but expressed complete faith that when the book was published, others would recognize as she had from the beginning the genius of Gertrude Stein. This faith grew when Gertrude let her read the scrawled pages of the unfinished *Making of Americans,* her long family history. Alice's faith in her strengthened Gertrude's faith in herself.

Since she had found no editors or publishers who wanted to publish *Three Lives* at their own risk, she had decided to pay for its publication herself. What was the use of a manuscript buried in a desk drawer!

The Grafton Press of New York finally agreed to print it. After they read the manuscript, far from recognizing genius, they suspected that the author wasn't educated, was not even at home in the English language, and must be a thoroughly confused person.

Gertrude was somewhat indignant but more amused when a young man, an American representing the Grafton Press in Paris, appeared at her door one day to see what manner of person this would-be author was. Upon meeting Miss Stein, he recognized at once her special quality and was more embarrassed than she was that his firm thought she needed checking on. Even so, the publisher in New York never did get used to her kind of prose and wrote her while the book was being printed, "I want to say frankly that you have written a very peculiar book and it will be a hard thing to make people take it seriously, but I want to assure you that I shall do all I can under the circumstances to please you."*

After all, he realized that this Miss Stein was having the book printed at her own expense, and if she refused to let him change a single word, cut out any of those endless repetitions, or improve her prose in any way, there was nothing he could do about it! She did, however, accept his one good suggestion that she change the title she had been using, *Three Histories*, to the less formal *Three Lives*, with the subtitle "Stories of the Good Anna, Melanctha, and the Gentle Lena."

Alice proved invaluable. She helped Gertrude carefully read the proofs of *Three Lives* as they arrived from New York at the Steins' home. Leo, too, was pleased to have Alice running in and out of 27, rue de Fleurus, not only because she took the burden of enthusiasm for Gertrude's writing off his reluctant shoulders but because she herself was good company.

As for Alice, she thought that frequently seeing the Steins made life "like a kaleidoscope slowly turning." Saturday nights in their studio were like bits of colored glass, constantly changing in hue and in pattern. Not only did the regulars like Picasso and Matisse come, but the curious from all corners of Paris, visiting art critics from England and other places, knocked on their door to say that "a friend of a friend" had told them that here they could see the new art.

* From *The Flowers of Friendship*, edited by Donald Gallup, by permission of Alfred A. Knopf, Inc.

One night the studio was full of Hungarians who had been sent by an enthusiastic fellow countryman. Another visitor was a Miss Mary Cassatt, an American living in France who, as a friend and disciple of Degas, had been invited years before to join and exhibit with the Impressionist. She had made quite a reputation for herself as a skillful and sensitive painter of mothers and children.

She and Gertrude Stein made a striking contrast. Miss Cassatt was a tall, spare spinster from Pennsylvania, quietly and elegantly dressed. Gertrude, who prided herself on being definitely of the twentieth century, sized up Miss Cassatt as the embodiment of the nineteenth. The one thing the two women discovered they had in common was that they had both been born in Allegheny, Pennsylvania. It amused them to recall how baffled French officials always were when they tried to spell or pronounce the name of their native city.

Throughout the evening Miss Cassatt looked stiff and uncomfortable in this crowd of gesticulating Bohemians. She was polite to her hostess but obviously pained at the sight of most of the avant-garde paintings. The one picture that seemed to hold her admiring attention was Cézanne's portrait of his wife. She left early without audible comment on anyone or anything, but her straight back was eloquent with disapproval.

That particular evening Leo had not felt called upon to lecture to the group. He had indigestion and sat with his feet high up on a bookcase—a remedy he had read about.

Alice was enjoying herself so much that she was among the last to leave. She had a long conversation about hats and perfumes with Picasso's beautiful Fernande, who had been giving her French lessons. And she promised Picasso himself that she would remind

Mlle Gertrude to save for him the next funny papers they got from America. He was particularly fond of the Katzenjammer Kids and did not want to miss any of them.

And so the kaleidoscope of life kept turning—summers in Fiesole, winters in Paris. Early in 1909, when Harriet Levy went back to the States, Gertrude, with Leo's consent, invited Alice to move into their *pavillon*. Leo was pleased that his sister would have Alice's companionship. It left him freer to pursue his new friendship with a fascinating woman, Nina Auzias. At first it was her experiences as a street singer and artist's model and her original and private thoughts that attracted his analytical mind. Then he found himself falling in love. Gertrude did not approve of any such liaison for her brother but was so immersed in writing her new book that she paid little attention to this affair of his.

Meanwhile *Three Lives* came out, making scarcely a ripple, let alone a big splash. Only a few discerning readers realized that in the story of Melanctha particularly, something new had appeared on the literary horizon. An unknown reviewer in the Kansas City *Star* came closest to understanding what this new writer Gertrude Stein was trying to do. "The originality of its narrative form is notable," he wrote. "As these human lives are groping in bewilderment, so does the story in telling itself." He spoke of the author's insistent repetition as making the book "a very masterpiece of realism."

Gertrude rejoiced over this unsolicited and understanding voice. "Melanctha," the story of the black woman, was proving the most successful of the three, being praised for its human, natural, and uncondescending portrayal of Negroes. James Weldon Johnson, a black poet, said that here was "the first white writer to write a story of love between a Negro man and woman and deal with them as normal members of the human family."

But Gertrude was disappointed that her adored Professor William James, to whom she had sent a copy, let her down. With great tact he wrote that he had read thirty or forty pages, thinking, "This is fine, a new kind of realism—Gertrude Stein is great." But it was clear that he was not able to finish the book. He added that she would see what a swine he was to have pearls cast before him. One time he had called on Gertrude in Paris. He gasped when he saw the paintings there and succeeded only in bringing out, "I always did tell you to keep an open mind."

Gertrude began to see more clearly that it was not going to be easy, being the author of a new kind of writing. A few, a very few, critics recognized her worth. She was pleased to get a complimentary letter from the famous H. G. Wells. But, for the most part, the world misunderstood or made fun of her, or, what was worse, ignored her completely. Some even felt that she was putting them on. Joking? Gertrude Stein? She was really never more serious in her life.

In October of 1911 Gertrude finally finished *Making of Americans*. It was such a long book that she had little hope of getting it published. For a respite from the long long book, she turned to writing psychological "portraits."

One Sunday evening she went into the kitchen, where Alice was using her talent to prepare one of her special dishes on the cook's night off. "Listen to this," Gertrude said. Then she read aloud the written portrait of "Ada," who turned out to be Alice herself. At first Alice was baffled, even wondering if Gertrude was making fun of her. But soon the felicitous phrases wove their magic on Alice and she realized that Gertrude had moved on into still another form of literature.

After that, there were word "portraits" of other friends—Matisse, Picasso, and later Mabel Dodge. Mrs. Dodge was so pleased and proud of hers that she had it printed, bound in Florentine paper, and distributed to influential people in Italy and back in the States.

Alfred Stieglitz, the master photographer, got hold of these Stein word portraits of Matisse and Picasso, publishing them in his magazine *Camera Work* in August 1912 along with illustrations of the artists' work.

These, too, baffled people. Bernard Berenson thanked Gertrude for the copy she sent him, saying about her prose, "It beats me hollow, and makes me dizzy to boot. So do some of the Picassos by the way. But I'll try try again."

When accused of being obscure and unnecessarily repetitious, Gertrude answered, "It is exactly like a frog hopping; he cannot ever hop exactly the same distance or the same way of hopping at every hop."

That was like Gertrude Stein. People would just have made up their minds that she was a sibyl, inscrutable and unintelligible. Then she would explain everything in the simple terms of a hopping frog. Few people knew that as a youngster in California she had watched and knew all about frogs jumping. That was the way she made her sentences move ahead.

In the summer of 1912 when she and Alice traveled together in Picasso's native Spain, they made quite a sensation in the villages. They did not mean to, but they did. Alice wore black to look as much as possible like the dignified and somber Spanish. Gertrude wore sandals and her voluminous brown robes that swirled about her as she moved along the dusty roads. Once when the two stopped to rest in the shade of a tree, a few villagers who had followed the pair of strangers came up to make obeisance, intending to kiss the ring of the imposing one they thought must be at least a bishop.

As in Italy, Gertrude became fascinated by the lives and personalities of the saints. A favorite was St. Teresa, who was born in Spain and whom Gertrude honored by putting her in *Four Saints in Three Acts* years later.

In Madrid at the bullfights Gertrude watched everything with keen interest while Alice shut her eyes tight when it looked as though man, horse, or bull might be hurt. Only when Gertrude said it was all right to look did Alice peek out again at the scene from under the rim of her black hat. On the other hand, it was Alice who became quite a fan and expert judge of Spanish dancing, attending all the dance recitals of sensational La Argentina.

While in Spain, Gertrude began to write short pieces inspired by Picasso's new approach to painting, now becoming known as cubism. On their return to Paris, Gertrude added to these short pieces and later grouped them under the title *Tender Buttons*. Here, for a change, Gertrude was not concerned with character but with objects, written about in ways completely intelligible to her and a few admirers but unintelligible to others.

Leo, who had already turned his back on Picasso's cubist paintings, now threw up his hands in dismay over Gertrude's new work. She resented his attitude, feeling that in cubism Picasso in paint and she in ink were both creating something new and important. Leo said "Tommyrot!" He had admired Picasso as a great painter of his age. He had loved Gertrude as a bright, entertaining companion all these years. But now he said frankly that what they were doing was "damned nonsense." He stopped going to the Saturday night receptions; he could

THEY NAMED ME GERTRUDE STEIN

no longer bear to "talk art" to the milling group of new-comers who were still welcomed by Gertrude. Fortunately, Alice was there to help and was particularly useful at overseeing refreshments and, as always, keeping the wives of artists amused while Gertrude entertained the artists themselves or promoted their works to visitors who might be persuaded to go out and buy the new art. Leo was no longer interested.

It became obvious to both brother and sister that the time had come to part. Leo took his share of the Renaissance furniture and his favorite paintings, particularly the Renoirs and some Cézannes, leaving Gertrude the ones she valued most highly and all the Picassos except a few of the early drawings. Off he went to Italy, still keeping in touch with his friend Nina through long philosophical letters.

Gertrude, less desolate than she might have expected, was left behind at 27, rue de Fleurus in what had become home. And if she no longer had Leo, she did have Alice.

She had other friends, too, people prominent in the arts who, very much impressed by Gertrude herself, worked hard to introduce her and her work to publishers. Mabel Dodge in America was talking to everyone about Gertrude Stein's writing. She said it was as ultramodern as the art in the famous—or infamous—Armory Show with its "Nude Descending a Staircase" that rocked New York early in 1913. Gertrude would have been more pleased with these efforts if she had not suspected that Mabel Dodge was even more interested in promoting Mabel Dodge. But when bright young men who read Gertrude's word portraits of Matisse and Picasso were going to Paris, they did ask Mabel Dodge for introductions to this new and exciting author.

One letter Gertrude received was an introduction to

Carl Van Vechten, the *New York Times* music critic and would-be novelist. Because he sounded promising, Gertrude wrote a note inviting him to dinner the following Saturday night.

Before then, in mid-week, she and Alice sat in a box at the Russian ballet, Stravinsky's *Sacre du Printemps* with choreography by Nijinsky. This ballet had caused an uproar on opening night, dividing all of Paris into two camps. Tonight again there were boos and hisses from one faction and shouts of "Bravo" from others in the audience. A late-comer into Gertrude's box was a handsome blond gentleman, elegant in evening clothes complete with the newest fashion in pleated shirts. Alice and Gertrude wondered about him but in the excitement of the uproar over the ballet could do no more than nod to the mysterious stranger.

Still, Gertrude could not forget him and on reaching home that night wrote a word portrait of the impressive young man which she called simply "One." Of course she was delighted when "One" proved to be their Saturday night dinner guest, Carl Van Vechten. For the rest of her life, he was one of her most loyal friends and admirers. Just as she had written a portrait of him, so he as a distinguished photographer later made countless portraits of her.

Gertrude was becoming better known now, at least among the few who kept up with the very latest in literature. She and Alice accepted an invitation to England and were welcomed at various weekend house parties where they kept meeting prominent and important people. But John Lane of The Bodley Head was the only editor who seemed at all interested in publishing an English edition of *Three Lives*. Gertrude pinned all her hopes on him.

It took him until the next year, on Gertrude's return

visit to London, to make up his mind, and then it was his American wife who persuaded him that *Three Lives* was a great find. That was in August 1914. It became more and more difficult to talk of books when everywhere, on every corner, in every drawing room, people talked only of war.

Gertrude and Alice were invited for the weekend to the country home of Alfred North Whitehead and his wife. It was on meeting the kindly and brilliant Dr. Whitehead that Alice said her inner bells began to peal, announcing her third genius. Gertrude, the American, had been her first; Picasso, the Spaniard, her second; and now this Englishman, Whitehead, the great philosopher, completed the trio.

While they were there, war was declared. The Germans invaded Belgium and began their drive on Paris. Gertrude was sick with anxiety and took refuge in her room. She scarcely gave a thought now to what would become of *Three Lives* or their apartment in Paris with its treasured paintings and manuscripts. She thought only of the city, of her beloved Paris and of its being ravaged by the enemy. She hardly dared believe it when the news came that the Germans had been stopped and Paris was saved, at least for the time being.

FIFTEEN

It was six weeks before it was considered safe enough for Gertrude and Alice to make the risky Channel crossing and go home. At first they tried to endure the wartime hardships of living in Paris. Gertrude sent her manuscripts to America for safekeeping and did what she could to protect the paintings. But frightening Zeppelin raids, shortages of food and light and heat, and increasing privations of all kinds plagued them day and night. In order to have more cash in hand Gertrude sold the "Femme au Chapeau," but it was bought by Sarah and Mike, who had wanted it from the beginning. So the notorious Matisse painting was still in the family.

A new Spanish painter, Juan Gris, whom Gertrude liked and tried to help, was almost destitute, since his Paris agent, a German, was in exile and all his pictures impounded. Picasso, being Spanish too, could not enlist, but all his friends were in the army. It was difficult to try to paint. Paris, though not occupied by the enemy, became so grim that Gertrude and Alice fled to Majorca to "forget the war a little."

It was impossible to forget completely and on their return to Paris in 1916 the two women abruptly gave up any attempt at detachment. One day in Paris they saw an American girl in uniform pull up in a car before a new office. Gertrude and Alice asked what she was doing. They decided then and there to do the same thing—

work for the American Fund for French wounded. They were told they would have to get a truck somehow and be prepared to deliver hospital supplies anywhere in France that they were most needed. Gertrude did not have a truck, did not even know how to drive. But those were small matters.

A cousin in New York sent her a Ford; an American friend who drove one of the old battle-of-the-Marne taxis taught her to drive. That is, he tried. On her first solo flight with only Alice by her side, Gertrude stalled between two streetcars. Everybody got out of the streetcars and pushed the truck and its two women off the track and over to the sidewalk. What could be the matter! Everybody took a hand at cranking the brand-new car, and nothing happened. Finally a shrewd onlooker guessed *pas d'essence.* He was right; there was no gas. Another constant hazard was that Gertrude never learned how to go into reverse. Going backward was not part of her nature. She and Alice called the car "Auntie" f ˜ Gertrude's Aunt Pauline, because "she behaved fairly well most times if she was properly flattered."

Their first important mission was to take desperately needed medical supplies all the way to Perpignan near the Spanish border and set up a depot there for future distribution. They drove through mud and snow, lost their way, had to be rescued several times from near-accidents. They picked up their first soldier hitchhiker. They called him their "military godson." Throughout the rest of the war they picked up dozens, scores, of military godsons who cheerfully changed or patched tires for the two oddly uniformed but interesting and talkative women, kept in touch with them by letter afterward, and generally felt they were extremely lucky to have met up with these angels of mercy. It was Gertrude who did the driving and most of the distributing; it was Alice who had the necessary interviews with officials and cut the red tape.

Then America came into the war. Gertrude was assigned to the town of Nîmes, where she and Alice rejoiced in seeing American doughboys. Gertrude asked every soldier she met who he was, where he was from, where his parents were from originally, what he did before the war, what he planned to do after the war, and how old he was. She reveled in their Americanism, and they in hers. She understood them all, whether their accents were of Kentucky or South Carolina or Iowa. And they understood her. When in a group they were asked to describe and pay tribute to a dead comrade, one young man said, "He had a heart as big as a washtub." He looked as though he thought Gertrude's heart was that big, too. She handed out "comfort bags" to them, full of small necessities that they found almost impossible to get—and cigarettes.

Finally there was the rejoicing over the Armistice, then some post-war work for civilian refugees in Alsace. Later, when the French government gave the two women the "Médaille de la Reconnaissance Française," they were pleased with the citation: "With grateful memories for your generous and devoted collaboration."

Now they were home again in Paris. As Gertrude often said, "America is my country; Paris is my home town." This might have sounded to some like divided allegiance, but it never was that, and after the war more than ever she combined America and France in her ardent affections.

Unfortunately, the old affection between Gertrude and Leo was a thing of the past. They seldom wrote to each other. Leo had sent one note from the States, where he had spent the war years. Now in 1919 he was back in Italy, feeling at the moment rather amiable toward his sister, and hopeful that his digestive troubles were cured. But his doubts and self-analysis continued. Gertrude still resented his scorn of her work. And when Leo finally married Nina, Gertrude and he made no further attempts to keep in touch with each other.

Gertrude would have been sad about it except that others, reading *Three Lives* as it was published in England or shorter pieces of hers that began to appear in little magazines, sought her out. In the old days, people came to 27, rue de Fleurus to see the pictures. Now in the next few years they came to see Gertrude.

The first and most welcome visitor was Sherwood Anderson, himself a writer of some renown in the States as the author of *Poor White* and *Winesburg, Ohio*. He asked Sylvia Beach, in her Paris bookshop "Shakespeare and Company," to give him an introduction to Miss Stein, whose writing he admired tremendously.

He told Gertrude quite simply how much her work meant to him. She was touched by this, and the two of them developed a firm and lasting friendship. Many of Gertrude's other "flowers of friendship" faded, but not hers with Anderson. Later, at her request, he did an introduction for her book *Geography and Plays* because she said, "You are really the only person who *really* knows what it is all about."

From America, Anderson sent a letter to Gertrude introducing Ernest Hemingway, an aspiring young writer. They took to each other at once—the good-looking, newly married young man, twenty-three years old, "with passionately interested" eyes, who sat at her feet as a pupil. And Gertrude, the teacher, a strikingly impressive woman of forty-eight with the "head of a Roman Emperor," who admitted she "had a weakness for Hemingway." She did not hesitate to tell him where his writing went off the track. "Begin over again and concentrate," she said. It was Alice's job to entertain Hemingway's wife, Hadley, during these writing conferences.

Gertrude tried to persuade the young man to leave his newspaper job as correspondent for the Toronto *Star* and concentrate on writing fiction. He wanted to but had no money; he couldn't quit his job because they were going to have a baby. He said he was too young to be a father! Reluctantly, he took his wife back to Canada, where he worked for the newspaper. But after the baby, "Bumby," came and they returned to Paris, Hemingway was charmed with this child who almost never cried, who watched with delight everything that happened around him and was never bored. Gertrude and Alice were pleased to be godmothers of John Hadley Hemingway. Alice, who had become skillful at needlepoint, covered a miniature chair for the baby, just as she made handsome chair seats and backs from Picasso designs for their own place on rue de Fleurus.

Gertrude told Hemingway of her *Making of Americans* and how disappointed she was that the thick manuscript had languished unpublished, unappreciated, locked up in her *armoire* for years. Hemingway read it, thought much of it magnificent, much of it repetitious, all of it overlong. But he, too, wished that it could be published somehow.

One day he burst into her place with the news that Ford Madox Ford was in Paris and wanted something of Gertrude Stein's for his new magazine called *Transatlantic* and Hemingway had persuaded him to start publishing *Making of Americans* serially. He had to have fifty pages right away for the next issue. It was very exciting! But there was only one copy on hand, and it was bound. Another copy was in the States going the rounds of publishers and being turned down. They

THEY NAMED ME GERTRUDE STEIN

couldn't take fifty pages out of the bound copy. What could they do!

Hemingway said, "I will type out fifty pages and get it to Ford at once." With Alice's help he did this and it was printed in the next number.

Gertrude was elated. She was convinced that her monumental work was really the beginning of modern writing. And here some of it, at least a small part of it, was in print at last.

In the long run, after many vicissitudes, the book fared better than did the friendship between Gertrude and Hemingway. Their relationship broke up finally for reasons that were never made very clear to outsiders, perhaps not entirely clear to each other. Some said that the rivalry between them became too great; some said that the friendship between them became so close that Alice objected. For whatever reason, the flowers of their friendship faded and died.

But for some time Gertrude and Hemingway admired and helped each other. In long conversations the older woman taught the young man much about how to use the natural rhythms of speech in his writing. How to use ordinary everyday words in what seemed like an ordinary way but was really extraordinary. Hemingway's devotion to Gertrude and his admiration of her and her work came at a time when she needed just such a young disciple. And of course she was always grateful to him for the launching of at least a small part of *Making of Americans*.

Other young men, including F. Scott Fitzgerald, came to pay homage to Gertrude Stein, and the place that Hemingway vacated was always filled by one or another member of what she was the first to call the "lost generation."

After the war Gertrude had bought a new Ford with

which to replace old, worn-out Auntie. The new one was a high two-seater. It came without any accessories—no cigarette lighter, no ash tray, no extras whatever. When Gertrude saw that the vehicle was completely unadorned, she called the car "Godiva."

One summer she and Alice drove Godiva to Antibes to visit Picasso. Fernande and he had long since parted. He was married now to Olga Khokhlova, a Russian ballet dancer from a good family who wanted him to be less bohemian and more bourgeois. For Paulot, their young son, Gertrude had written *A Birthday Book* because his birthday was February 4, one day after her own.

Another summer, on their way again to the Picassos', Gertrude and Alice in Godiva pulled up short in the town of Belley in front of the delightful Hotel Pernollet, gay with flower boxes across the front. Intending to stay a night or two only, they liked everything so much that they never did get on to Picasso's place on the Riviera. They liked the hotel, the cordial family who ran the place, M. and Mme Pernollet. They found the local *spécialités* delicious—they were a fish called lavaret, and the white wine of the region, called "Seysal." They were delighted by their walks and drives in the hilly countryside with its charming gardens and clear mountain air. Here in the valley of the Rhone was a region that suited them perfectly.

In the next two summers, on their return to Belley and on their excursions in Godiva into the green and fertile valley, they had a definite purpose. It was to find the perfect house they could rent in future summers, a house where Alice could supervise a garden of flowers and vegetables and exercise her talents in the kitchen; a house where Gertrude could have a study for her writing, and where they could entertain all their friends. The houses they liked were not for sale or, if for sale, they had too little water. Nothing they saw for rent had furnishings that appealed to them at all. They couldn't imagine living with the pictures on those walls.

But one afternoon from across the valley they saw the house of their dreams. It was high on a hill, built of stone, somewhat stately but not overwhelming, large but not too large, even somehow cozy, fitting serenely and with perfect composure into its surroundings of green, and flanked by charming turrets on what must be a walled terrace.

In great excitement they returned to town and found the agent for the house, only to be told that the house was neither for sale nor for rent. The man who had a long-term lease on it was perfectly happy renting the house and no doubt would be there for years with his family. He was a captain in the army, his garrison was at Belley. A perfect arrangement. No, of course he and his family could not be evicted! Surely the American ladies could find another house they liked as well.

But they knew they couldn't and they didn't. Together Gertrude and Alice concocted a scheme. If only their captain were promoted and then transferred, everybody would be happy. On their return to Paris, they pulled strings, they talked to influential friends in the army. Gertrude was not averse to reminding them of her services to the French wounded in the war. The captain was given the opportunity to come up to Versailles and take exams for promotion. He took them and failed them. After three months, he tried again. Again he failed. It looked as though he would always remain a captain and would always remain in their dream house. Eventually a solution was found. Gertrude and Alice were never sure whether it was due to their efforts or not, but finally the captain was offered a post in Africa at greatly increased pay. He accepted.

The two women were delighted and in the spring of '29 with a white poodle puppy moved into the house that they had never seen up close. They found it completely charming, even better than they had imagined: the house itself, the terrace with its yellow tulips and borders of boxwood, and best of all the breath-taking view of the hills beyond and the valley below from which they had first glimpsed their treasure!

Meanwhile, another dream of Gertrude's had come true. *Making of Americans* was published in France in 1925 by Contact Editions, printed by the same French printer who had done James Joyce's *Ulysses*. But there were flaws in this dream. There were too few copies printed, there was too little publicity, there was inadequate distribution, too many arguments with the publisher, and too few sales to make the book a big success.

And it was not until 1934 that the enormous book, reduced to 416 pages, was brought out in America, where all along Gertrude thought it belonged. *Making of Americans* had taken her between five and eight years to write. She had finished it in 1911. It took almost fourteen years to get it published in France. It took more than twenty years to get an abridged edition published in America. Gertrude always felt that this was her masterpiece. Now even while she rejoiced, she thought it ironic that it was published in New York only because the year before, 1933, she had dashed off in six weeks a short best seller, *The Autobiography of Alice B. Toklas*.

SIXTEEN

Gertrude kept saying that Alice should write her own memoirs. She could call it something like "Wives of Geniuses I Have Sat with" or "My Twenty-five Years with Gertrude Stein." But Alice always protested. If she ever wrote a book, it would probably be a cookbook. She was far too busy typing for Gertrude, gardening and embroidering, and supervising the kitchen and taking care of the dogs, to write about her own life. Besides, she knew better than anyone that whatever light she might shed on their lives in Paris or in the countryside would only be a reflection of Gertrude's own more powerful light.

And so *The Autobiography of Alice B. Toklas* was finally written by Gertrude. A tour de force perhaps, but in an honorable tradition—almost that of *Tom Sawyer* or *Robinson Crusoe*. Here was Gertrude taking on the role of Alice. This had some disadvantages but more advantages. For instance, Gertrude could not have called herself a genius; that would be too blatant. But it was natural enough if she were writing as Alice to have her say, as she actually had said, "A bell within me rang when I met my first genius, Gertrude Stein." Best of all from the reader's point of view, the book proved to be written in a way that was not cryptic, esoteric, repetitious, or tangential. This time the author was not the baffling Gertrude Stein, she was the unexpectedly clear, forthright, amusing, and gossiping Gertrude Stein pretending to be Alice B. Toklas.

Everyone bought the book; everyone loved it. That is, everyone loved it who was not more or less gently kicked in the shins by the author. The Matisses, whom Gertrude really admired, took offense at her remark about Mme Matisse's having a "long face and a firm large loosely hung mouth like a horse." Picasso's wife Olga resented the amount of space given to the beautiful Fernande. André Gide could not have been pleased to read that, when he turned up, "it was a rather dull evening." Ezra Pound must have felt put down when he was dismissed as a "village explainer." Her reference to Hemingway as "90% Rotarian" was not by any means the worst thing Gertrude called him in the book. It must have been disconcerting to Glenway Westcott to read of himself that "he has a certain syrup but it does not pour." Leo found nothing in the book that was insulting to him, unless it was the fact that he was scarcely mentioned at all. But he felt that Gertrude had frivolously changed too many facts into fancy and that what she had written was an extravagant "romance." A group of people including Matisse issued a pamphlet charging Gertrude with inaccuracies, ignorance of art, and an inadequate knowledge of French.

But almost everyone else was enthusiastic about the book. It was much more than just chitchat; it was a colorful, skillfully drawn portrait of Paris in an exciting time, an intimate portrait of herself and of future greats, and if Gertrude included herself among the greats, she did it in a most entertaining and disarming way. With publication of the book in 1933, Americans grew better acquainted with Gertrude Stein. She had long hoped to become famous through her serious writing. Instead, she now found herself famous because of a popular best seller, a book dashed off in six weeks, tongue in cheek, as an "autobiography" of someone else.

Until now her books had been read only by the knowledgeable few. But thanks mostly to Carl Van Vechten's enthusiastic promotion, even those who had not read her knew something of her unusual style of writing. They could quote with amusement, "rose is a rose is a rose is a rose," even though they had never dipped into her *Geography and Plays,* where the line first appeared.

They knew what Gertrude Stein looked like, too, because of several portraits by modern artists and the fine pieces of sculpture that Lipchitz and Jo Davidson had done of her in the twenties. Later she had her crown of hair cut off, but close-cropped her head made her look even more distinguished. Sherwood Anderson said she looked like a monk. Picasso, after a moment of anxiety about whether she would still be the woman of his portrait, said in relief, "It is all there." She had begun to dress with more flair, too, adopting a style that was peculiarly her own—wearing a wardrobe of handsome embroidered waistcoats over blouses with good-looking antique cuff links, and the same wide skirts but of better material and better cut. Sometimes she donned one of her colorful Chinese coats.

Now, thanks to the *Autobiography,* she was fast becoming a celebrity.

Her reputation was clinched by a fantastic performance of an opera she had written for Virgil Thomson; he had put his music to her words in *Four Saints in Three Acts.* With much advance ballyhoo, the première was given in February 1934 in Hartford, Connecticut, in the theater of a new wing of the museum there. Everyone who was anyone went, from New York and Boston and Philadelphia and even Chicago, for opening night. There was an all-black cast singing magnificently; there were stage settings the like of which had never been seen before, made of cellophane, feathers, glass beads, shells, and lace. The music was marvelously new. What of the libretto? What of Gertrude Stein's words concerning Saint Teresa and Saint Ignatius? To some they were incomprehensible. There was no plot as such, no story. But for those who listened as they would listen to a stirring oratorio and for those who looked as they would look at beautiful tableaux or ballets, the performance was a triumph. It moved on to Broadway, where it was an overnight popular success.

From this opera Gertrude Stein's followers picked up new lines to say. "Pigeons on the grass, alas" and "Magpie in the sky" became quotes as well known as "rose is a rose is a rose."

Van Vechten and others asked if it weren't high time that Gertrude Stein came back to enjoy for herself her new fame in her homeland. When in the fall of 1934 she was invited to lecture at colleges from New England to California, she accepted. She said, "I always did want to go back as a lion, and now I am."

She had done a little lecturing at Oxford and Cambridge back in 1926. Then she had had stage fright, until she discovered that lecturing wasn't different from talking to people. She had a success with both students and professors in England. But how would it be in America?

On the ship crossing, she had moments of panic, feeling less like a lion than like a lamb being led to slaughter. After all, she had stayed away for thirty years. What if her own countrymen didn't welcome her? All doubts fled, however, for when the ship dropped anchor off New York she was lionized by reporters and photographers who came out in the press launch to meet her. One of them was a favorite doughboy friend from war days, W. G. Rogers, now an editor in Massachusetts. With

Rogers at her elbow and Alice hovering in the background, she held an impromptu news conference and with great good humor answered questions. One young man, impressed by her clear answers, said, "Why don't you write the way you talk?" She countered, "Why don't you read the way I write?" When they asked her about all those repetitions, she made them laugh by saying, "No, no, no, no it is not all repetition."

Most of the afternoon news stories tried to imitate her writing with such headlines as "Gerty Gerty Stein Stein." But it was all very good-natured and *The New York Times* put her name in electric lights that moved like a bright ribbon around the Times building announcing her arrival. Gertrude was gratified. She really was coming in like a lion. She laughed her heartiest when she heard the newly popular limerick:

> There's a notable family called Stein:
> There's Gertrude, there's Ep, and there's Ein.
>   Gertrude's writings are punk,
>   Ep's statues are junk,
> And nobody understands Ein.

Being lampooned in a rhyme like this, which was quoted everywhere and later immortalized within the sacred covers of Bartlett's *Familiar Quotations,* she knew she had arrived.

From October until May, Gertrude breathed deep of America and felt at home wherever she went. Before her lectures in New York, New England, the South, and the West, she walked along the streets and on the campuses, genuinely touched when greeted by name by strangers everywhere—all kinds of people from the man at a fruit stand in New York to a shy freshman on a Midwestern college green.

She had laid down only one requirement: she would

lecture to no more than five hundred people at a time, saying that that was enough, when her lectures would be difficult for her to read and difficult for others to listen to. She meant it, too. She refused to appear at her first Columbia Extension lecture until half of the thousand people who wanted to hear her were turned away. News of this was enough to whet the appetite of audiences everywhere.

A typical scene unfolded at Brown University and its sister institution, Pembroke College, when students, faculty, and the townspeople of Providence clamored for the five hundred numbered tickets that were doled out. Of course, many of the five hundred came out of curiosity. What would she be like in person—this woman who had been hailed by the reverent in Paris and New York as "the genius of twentieth-century literature" but also by the irreverent as "the Great Stone Face" and even "the Covered Wagon"? Some of the university skeptics came to scoff. What could she tell English majors and professors about "Grammar and Poetry"? She told them; she told them a lot.

The newspaper columnist B. K. Hart reported in the Providence *Journal* next day:

She spoke in accents neither wild nor confused but with an idiom that was crisp, skimped of adjectives, pleased with the adverb and the preposition, more than partisan to the conjunctions.

So avid was the curiosity of the public to see this extraordinary authoress that almost a small riot developed outside the windows. . . . Literally hundreds were turned away and all evening long valiant scores stood in the dripping night with their faces pressed to the window-panes to watch the woman who upset the whole apple-cart of grammar. . . . We had expected, all of us, to see something . . . that perhaps Barnum would have bought for his circus. We were pleasantly disappointed. Stocky, rugged, forthright, planted squarely on the stage and speaking in a crisp accent with most (but not all) of her periods quite lucid, she promptly won the hearts of her audience in such a manner that a genial glow seemed to pass back and forth between her and her listeners, until we became all good little pals together, examining a new adventure into the mystery-land of words.

She gave aid and comfort to those students who always had trouble with punctuation. Among other things, she said, "What is the use of a question-mark in any case? If I asked a question and you didn't know it was a question I don't see what use the question would be to you anyway."

She felt strongly about commas, too, maintaining that commas were only a signal that the reader should pause and take a breath. But the reader himself should have sense enough to know when he wanted to take a breath. Commas were really unnecessary.

B. K. Hart went on with his account:

We all gathered around in a huge salon afterwards. She signed books for us, answered questions briskly and even when she tried to leave (she was bound by night train for Springfield) the whole mob of us followed in her wake.

This scene was repeated in place after place. At Harvard and Radcliffe, too, she was a success, but there Gertrude felt that things had changed so much since she had lived in Cambridge as an undergraduate that it wasn't at all the place she remembered. She missed the faculty she had known. Professor James had died years before; all the familiar faces were gone.

Gertrude was excited and afraid at the prospect of her first flight in a plane. When invited to Chicago to see a performance of her *Four Saints in Three Acts*, she declined because she couldn't get there in time on a train. What about taking a plane? That was impossible, she said, because she never had and she was afraid to fly. Carl Van Vechten, her American guardian, said, "Nonsense. It will be all right. I'll go with you." From the minute they took off, Gertrude loved flying. It was even more exciting than seeing her own opera on the stage. She liked looking down on the countryside so neatly divided into squares that it looked like a series of cubist paintings.

After that, she and Alice flew everywhere. They spent Christmas with relatives in Baltimore; farther south, they were charmed by the fragrance of early flowers; in Washington they were invited by Mrs. Roosevelt to tea in the White House; in California they revisited childhood scenes and met Hollywood writers and actors; in Chicago, Gertrude held a series of special seminars with bright university students chosen by her new friends Thornton Wilder and President Robert Hutchins.

In one seminar, students asked what she meant by "rose is a rose is a rose." They thought her explanation made good sense.

"Now listen," she said. "Can't you see that when the language was new—as it was with Chaucer and Homer —the poet could use the name of a thing and the thing was really there. He could say 'O moon,' 'O sea,' 'O love,' and the moon and the sea and love were really there. And can't you see that after hundreds of years had gone by and thousands of poems had been written, he could call on those words and find that they were just worn-out literary words. . . . Now the poet has to get back that intensity into language. . . . It's not enough to be bizarre; the strangeness in the sentence structure has to come from the poetic gift, too. . . . Now you all have seen hundreds of poems about roses and you know in your bones that a rose is not there. . . . But I notice that you all know [my line]; you make fun of it but you know it. Now listen! I'm no fool. I know that in daily life we don't go around saying '. . . is a . . . is a . . . is a. . . .' Yes, I'm no fool; but I think that in that line the rose is red for the first time in English poetry for a hundred years."*

Finally the lectures, the classes, the visits, and the interviews were all over. Back in New York, Gertrude found that Bennett Cerf wanted to sign her up for new books—one of which would be an account of her recent experiences in America, to be called *Everybody's Autobiography*. This delighted her. Then there were all the farewells, and on May 4, 1935, Gertrude and Alice sailed for France.

On the voyage they wrote thank-you letters to their many American friends—old and new. To a student at the University of California, Gertrude wrote, "My dear Bowie, Here we are on our way back and we did have a good time over there, we knew it while we were having it and we know it now that we have had it and not the least of it was with you all. . . ."

When they landed in France, where the old life was to begin again, Gertrude knew that this time there would be a difference. She had rediscovered her homeland and knew more certainly than ever that she would always belong to America, even though she still called Paris her home town.

* From Thornton Wilder's introduction to Gertrude Stein's *Four in America*, by permission of Yale University Press.

SEVENTEEN

For a while the old life did continue. Paris in the winters, Bilignin in the summers, writing, always writing, walking along the Seine, above the valley or in the hills, enjoying the companionable dogs—Basket, the white poodle, and Pépé, the small black chihuahua given to her by Picabia, the painter—constantly entertaining artists, writers, friends from everywhere: this made up Gertrude's life. And always there was Alice to smooth the way, to do the typing, to arrange entertainment for the guests, to protect Gertrude from too many interruptions, to supervise the procession of cooks, and in her few hours of idleness to embroider in a circle on fine household linens the well-known device, "rose is a rose is a rose is a rose." If Alice was always somewhat in the background, it was because she chose to be there and manage things from behind the scenes.

When, in 1938, the landlord at 27, rue de Fleurus claimed the apartment for his son's family, the two women packed up their belongings and the precious paintings, including those by Gertrude's new discovery, Sir Francis Rose, and moved cheerfully enough to a conveniently arranged apartment nearby, at 5, rue Christine. As Gertrude said in her little book *Paris, France,* "anywhere one lives is interesting and beautiful." Around the corner was Picasso's new apartment.

For a time, however, Gertrude was not on friendly

terms with Picasso. He had stopped painting and took to writing what he hopefully called poetry. Gertrude thought this a terrible waste of his true talents and said so. It took him many months to come around to her way of thinking. But finally he gave up playing with words and went back to working at his easel. Gertrude rejoiced and wrote a short book about him and his work, called simply *Picasso*. She wrote it first in French, asking Alice to correct any grammatical errors, then in English, and it was a success in both languages. The *Manchester Guardian* said, "Miss Stein writes exactly as she thinks and she thinks by instinct and after all that is how Picasso paints so why shouldn't that be a good way of explaining Picasso . . . ?"

Life might have gone on indefinitely in this way, peacefully and productively for Gertrude, but she saw, everyone saw, war clouds beginning to hide the sun once more. Once again Germany was the enemy, but this time it was Hitler's Nazi Germany. This time it would be different. Gertrude and Alice were in Bilignin in September 1939 when war was declared, and Gertrude uttered a cry of anguished disbelief and protest.

Because Mike and Sarah had moved back to the States, there was no one now in Paris who could take care of Gertrude's paintings. She and Alice got thirty-six-hour passes to make one brief dash in their car up to Paris. From their apartment they gathered together a few necessities such as winter clothing and had a hurried conference over what to do with the paintings. Obviously they must make room in the car to take back to the country for safekeeping Picasso's portrait of Gertrude and Cézanne's portrait of his wife. But what to do with the others! Putting them on the apartment floor now might save them from being hurled off the walls later in an air raid. But the one floor would not hold all those from the four walls. And there was no time, no time at all to plan.

They went back to Bilignin, where country quiet calmed them for the time being. The only news of the outside world came over their new radio. Gertrude listened every day. For a long while, nothing happened. The French believed that the Maginot Line would protect them. On the radio there was only music, constant music, that she felt as harassing as any enemy in this war that was not yet a fighting war.

Out-of-doors in the early winter evenings, Gertrude walked the country roads for exercise with young Basket II, successor to the old Basket, who had been so named because Gertrude had said he looked as though he should carry a basket of flowers in his mouth. In the light of the rising moon the large bulky figure of this foreign neighbor became a familiar sight to the farm families in the area. She greeted everyone warmly as she passed, stopping to chat a minute before striding on down the road with the shaggy white unclipped poodle by her side. The children affectionately called him the "dog in pajamas." Whatever happened, they were all in this together—old farmers, animals, children, and the American ladies who were for the first time living in the neighborhood all year round.

In the spring the army gave young farmers agricultural leave to come back to plant the fields. Alice again dug and planted the vegetable garden, which this time would make the difference between hunger and plenty.

May was a month of disaster for France. May was the month when the king of the Belgians surrendered, the month of the swift invasion by the Germans, who rolled around the Maginot Line over Sedan and Amiens and on toward the sea. The British, in anything large or small that would float, rescued at Dunkirk 260,000 of

Leo, Gertrude, and Michael Stein (left to right) *in the courtyard of 27, rue de Fleurus, about 1906* THE BALTIMORE MUSEUM OF ART, CONE COLLECTION

Gertrude Stein behind the wheel of a Red Cross truck, 1917. Alice B. Toklas stands on the sidewalk COLLECTION OF AMERICAN LITERATURE, BEINECKE LIBRARY, YALE UNIVERSITY

Gertrude Stein with her dogs, Basket and Pepe, on the terrace of her villa in Bilignin, 1934 ESTATE OF CARL VAN VECHTEN

Gertrude Stein and Alice B. Toklas, holding good-luck charms given them by Hopi Indians, board a plane for their first flight, 1934 ESTATE OF CARL VAN VECHTEN

Gertrude Stein surrounded by students after her lecture at the College of William and Mary, 1935 ESTATE OF CARL VAN VECHTEN

Gertrude Stein having tea with American G Is (her dog Basket in foreground), *1945* COLLECTION OF AMERICAN LITERATURE, BEINECKE LIBRARY, YALE UNIVERSITY

their own men and 90,000 French, taking them back to England to reassemble. Paris fell to the enemy. It was not defended against the invaders; defense would have been futile and would have meant destruction of the city. As one correspondent said, "Even Joan of Arc couldn't have stopped tanks with a pea shooter."

As yet, none of the terrible fighting was anywhere near Belley. But Gertrude suffered as she listened to the sad and bitter reports that came over the radio. When in June Mussolini declared war on France, that seemed the last straw. Italy was no longer the Italy that Gertrude had known and loved as a girl. Now Italy too was the enemy, now Belley was directly in the path of any troop movements from the south as well as from the north.

They did not often speak of it, but Gertrude and Alice were very much aware that being Jewish and being foreign as well made them especially vulnerable. Grimly, silently, the very shadow and threat of concentration camps fell across their daily lives. They could be seized at any time by Hitler's soldiers; they could be denounced by any German sympathizer, by a neighbor even. What would become of them?

When they went to Lyon to ask the American consul what to do, he urged them to leave at once for Spain, for Switzerland, for any neutral country where they would be safe. The two women discussed it. Should they be prudent and go? Or should they stay and brave it out?

In an agony of indecision they consulted Doctor and Madame Chaboux, who urged that they stay in Bilignin, right where they were, among friends, and not risk hazards of the unknown among strangers.

This was just what Gertrude needed, what she hoped to hear. It gave her the courage to be courageous. She and Alice decided they would try to stick it out, and they did. Later, when the region was invaded and the Germans in their gray uniforms were everywhere on the streets of Belley, the mayor deliberately neglected to put the names of Stein and Toklas on the lists of inhabitants that he had to turn over to the intruders. No one ever denounced them or gave the two names to the despised enemy. Jewish the two ladies might be, but first of all they were friends and neighbors.

Blackouts were ordered for every household. Shutters were closed tight every evening at dusk. Curfews were strictly imposed, and Gertrude could no longer walk the country roads after dark. Instead, she paced back and forth on the terrace, making up stories for children that she hoped to write. That seemed one of the few ways to escape for a little while the confinement and the menace of the war. In cold weather, another way was to saw wood for the kitchen stove and open hearth. There was no other heat in the big stone house. The exercise with the saw and later the burning wood made Gertrude feel twice warmed. In the evening she sat by the fire, reading or writing, while Alice knitted socks for the neighborhood boys gone off to war. Post-office service was completely disrupted; no letters came and none could be sent. So, instead of writing letters, Gertrude wrote down the stories for children.

In 1943 their lease on the house in Bilignin expired and the owner, an officer in the now almost disbanded French army, claimed the house for himself and his family. Gertrude was losing her dream house, the house she had discovered and loved and called home for so many summers. She was terribly upset; she had no choice but to move into a place outside the town of Culoz nearby.

The house, called "la Colombière," old and gray and with a graceful roof, was situated on a hill in a park beside a clear stream that ran down from the mountain and through the town. The lease included two servants.

THEY NAMED ME GERTRUDE STEIN

The new cook, however, proved to be no help at all. She said she could not cook without butter or cream or eggs; so Alice, with much ingenuity, prepared the meals. The two exiles settled in comfortably enough, having brought with them such personal conveniences as a water heater and a bathtub. They tried not to look back with too much regret on older and happier days in the older and happier place.

One night in the summer of that year Basket barked a warning and there came a knocking on the door. A German officer demanded quarters for his men. Gertrude asked, "Do you have a paper from the mayor?" When he assured her that he had, she sent him around to the back door, where he gave the servants orders demanding two rooms for officers and six mattresses for the men. He would not take no for an answer, he said, and never mind the lady of the house! "Very well, sir," said the servants; and when the officer left, they began arranging everything with Gertrude's help. They hid some of their food supplies and valuables. Then Gertrude and Alice and Basket retreated to the upstairs. Gertrude thought it wiser not to talk to the Germans herself, for fear her American accent might betray her. The German soldiers who came in were more agreeable than their commander. In the end there were fifteen men sleeping on six mattresses. Two of their three dogs slept on the floor; the third dog refused to come in. When the men finally left at the end of two weeks they carried off the new slippers of one of the servants, all the peaches that had been stored away, and the keys to both the front and back doors. Their third dog who wouldn't come in wouldn't go off with them either; so he became part of the household.

Apparently the Germans had arrived in Culoz to fight the *maquis*, the young men of the Resistance movement, patriots loyal to France, who hid in the mountains and descended every night to harass the enemy, blowing up bridges, chopping down trees with which to block roads, planting mines, and generally creating confusion. The *maquis* were hard to fight because they were hard to find. The sound of gunfire and explosions all around her cheered Gertrude; she thought the *maquis* were wonderful.

Each day she wrote up that day's events in her notebooks, her diary, which eventually she called *Wars I Have Seen*. Alice began typing it. Gertrude said, "I'll finish it the day the Americans come."

The Americans landed first in the north in June 1944 on Normandy's beaches. Like everyone else, almost more than anyone else, Gertrude was wild with impatience to welcome them. To keep busy and to feel that she was doing something, she spent hours weeding the terrace so that Americans could sprawl on a neat lawn when they arrived. Alice checked over her hoarded supplies of raisins, nuts, and candied fruits for a magnificent Liberation cake for her victorious fellow countrymen.

On August 14, when Gertrude heard Eisenhower's announcement of the American landings in the south on the Mediterranean beaches, she sang, "Glory hallelujah!" Pursuing the enemy up the valley of the Rhone, the Americans soon reached Grenoble. Only eighty kilometers away! Then Aix-les-Bains, only twenty-five kilometers—and nothing now except a few pockets of the enemy between them and Culoz and Belley. How soon would they come? Over the radio the news came that Paris was freed and all of France rejoiced.

Then, on September 1, Gertrude wrote in her diary, "Oh happy day, that is all I can say oh happy day," for Americans arrived in Belley and Culoz. Gertrude embraced them, rode in an American jeep, and brought home with her a lieutenant colonel and a private to sleep in the beds the Germans had occupied such a short time before.

And the next day Eric Sevareid and Frank Gervasi with other journalists, Price Day of the Baltimore *Sun* and Newbold Noyes of the Washington *Star,* arrived to "liberate" poor, seventy-year-old Gertrude Stein. They found her indomitable and deliriously happy. Again she embraced her fellow Americans, had them stay for a delicious victory lunch, and wore them out with eager questions about America, talking and laughing in the voice that the men thought was as rich and smooth as the fresh cream the household had been without for so long. As they left and Gervasi said that he would be flying back to the States, Gertrude entrusted him with her manuscript to take to Bennett Cerf—the diary she had joyfully ended that very day with "the war is over and this certainly is the last war to remember."

Underneath their jubilation over victory, Gertrude and Alice began to feel a gnawing anxiety about the fate of their Paris apartment and the paintings they had left behind. Had they been harmed in any way or stolen by the Germans? It wasn't until November that word came from a neighbor that just two weeks before the occupying Germans had left the city, four men of the Gestapo had forced their way into the apartment and made such a disturbance that the young woman from the book bindery on the first floor rushed upstairs to investigate. She banged on the locked door until the intruders, to keep her quiet, let her come in. They were in a fury, shaking their fists at the Picassos, threatening to slash and burn such filth. On recognizing the Francis Rose portrait of Gertrude, they grew even more violent, saying they would burn it, they would burn all such Jews. The girl could do nothing with them herself, so she rushed downstairs again and telephoned the police.

In no time the commissaire himself and thirty police were on hand, finding the men in the bedroom roughly handling and trying on Gertrude's Chinese coats. When the commissaire found the intruders had not brought a search warrant, he ordered them out. They went but took the key with them, obviously intending to return. The girl stood staunchly by the door until someone called a locksmith, who came and changed the lock.

Gertrude and Alice were quite shaken by this account. But the pictures were saved and that was what mattered!

They themselves did not go back to Paris until December. Gertrude was asked to broadcast to America and was flown to various army bases to talk to the troops. Her talks had serious overtones. When the joyous mood of victory had calmed down somewhat, Gertrude spoke to the soldiers about some of the problems ahead. Among other things, she said that they would all go home and stand in line to get jobs making gadgets, to make money so that they could all stand in line to buy them.

Settling down in Paris, Gertrude began writing again but was constantly besieged by Americans who wanted to meet her, wanted to see her paintings, wanted to ask her advice, wanted to hear her talk and laugh in the way they had heard about from so many. Janet Flanner, who wrote from Paris for *The New Yorker*, said, "Gertrude Stein's laugh was one of the most warming human sounds I ever heard. It was a kindling laugh, like the rumble of a country stove."

Those two years after the war were tiring. All the writing, the many callers, all the post-war duties and problems began to wear her down. They did not affect her courageous spirit so much as they did her weakening

THEY NAMED ME GERTRUDE STEIN

body. Suddenly she was not at all well and a doctor, suspecting cancer, urged her to see a specialist. She refused. Perhaps she knew that it was already too late.

When finally she was forced to go to the hospital, the doctors had many consultations. Should they operate? Or was it hopeless? Gertrude had several days lying in a white hospital bed in which to ponder both her life and her approaching death. Did she remember that as a young girl she had searched anxiously for some assurance of eternal life? Now, on this last troubled afternoon before surgery, she murmured, partly to Alice, partly to herself, and partly to the unknown ahead of her, "What is the answer?" When there was only silence, she asked quietly, "In that case, what is the question?"

Perhaps she remembered and was comforted by something she had thought and written during the perilous days of the war: "These days nobody minds death from fear of heaven or hell but there is there always is with death the cessation of life and life is interesting."

Yes, no matter what the answer or what the question, life had always been interesting to Gertrude Stein.

BIBLIOGRAPHY

BAKER, CARLOS: *Ernest Hemingway: A Life Story.* N.Y.: Scribner, 1969.

BARR, ALFRED J.: *Matisse: His Art and His Public.* N.Y.: Museum of Modern Art, 1952.

BIDDLE, GEORGE: *An American Artist's Story.* Boston: Little, Brown, 1939.

BIZARDEL, YVON: *American Painters in Paris.* N.Y.: Macmillan, 1960.

————: *Sous l'Occupation: Souvenirs d'un conservateur de musée 1940–1944.* Paris: Calmann-Lévy, 1964.

BERENSON, BERNARD: *Rumor and Reflection.* N.Y.: Simon & Schuster, 1952.

————: *The Selected Letters of Bernard Berenson,* A. K. McComb, ed. Boston: Houghton Mifflin, 1963.

BRIDGMAN, RICHARD: *Gertrude Stein in Pieces.* N.Y.: Oxford University Press, 1970.

BRINNIN, JOHN MALCOLM: *The Third Rose: Gertrude Stein and Her World.* London: Weidenfeld & Nicolson, 1960.

BOWLES, PAUL: *Without Stopping.* N.Y.: Putnam, 1972.

CHAMBERLAIN, SAMUEL: *Fair Harvard.* Cambridge: Harvard University Press, 1948.

COGNIAT, RAYMOND: *Cézanne.* N.Y.: Crown, 1968.

CRESPELLE, JEAN-PAUL: *Picasso and His Women.* N.Y.: Coward McCann, 1969.

FLANNER, JANET: *Paris Journal,* Vol. I, 1944–1965. N.Y.: Atheneum, 1965.

————: *Paris Journal,* Vol. II, 1965–1971. N.Y.: Atheneum, 1971.

Four Americans in Paris. N.Y.: Museum of Modern Art, 1970.

GALLUP, DONALD CLIFFORD, ed.: *The Flowers of Friendship: Letters Written to Gertrude Stein.* N.Y.: Knopf, 1953.

————: *The Making of Making of Americans*. N.Y.: Duschnes Crawford, 1950.

GILOT, FRANÇOISE, AND LAKE, CARLTON: *Life with Picasso*. N.Y.: McGraw-Hill, 1964.

GRATTAN, C. HARTLEY: *The Three Jameses*. N.Y.: Longmans, Green & Co., 1932.

HARRISON, GILBERT A., ed.: *Gertrude Stein's America*. Washington, D.C.: Robert B. Luce, Inc., 1965.

HEMINGWAY, ERNEST: *A Moveable Feast*. N.Y.: Scribner, 1964.

HILLAIRET, JACQUES: *Dictionnaire historique des rues de Paris*. Paris: Editions de Minuit, 1961.

IMBS, BRAVIG: *Confessions of Another Young Man*. N.Y.: The Henkle-Yewdale House, Inc., 1936.

JAFFÉ, HANS: *Picasso*. Twentieth Century Masters. London: Hamlyn, 1970.

JOLAS, EUGENE AND MARIA: *Testimony Against Gertrude Stein*. Paris, 1935.

KAZIN, ALFRED: *On Native Grounds*. N.Y.: Harcourt Brace, 1942.

LUHAN, MABEL DODGE: *European Experiences*. N.Y.: Harcourt Brace, 1935.

MARIANO, NICKY: *Forty Years with Berenson*. N.Y.: Knopf, 1966.

MAUROIS, ANDRÉ: *A History of France*. London: Jonathan Cape, 1952.

MILLER, ROSALIND S.: *Gertrude Stein: Form and Intelligibility*. N.Y.: Exposition Press, 1949.

MORISON, SAMUEL ELIOT: *Three Centuries of Harvard*. Cambridge: Harvard University Press, 1936.

OLIVIER, FERNANDE: *Picasso and His Friends*. N.Y.: Appleton-Century, 1965.

PERRUCHOT, HENRI: *Cézanne*. Translated by Humphrey Hare. N.Y.: World, 1961.

POLLACK, BARBARA: *The Collectors: Dr. Claribel and Miss Etta Cone*. N.Y.: Bobbs-Merrill, 1962.

PUTNAM, SAMUEL: *Paris Was Our Mistress*. N.Y.: Viking, 1947.

REWALD, JOHN: *Paul Cézanne: A Biography*. N.Y.: Schocken Books, 1968.

ROGERS, W. G.: *When This You See Remember Me: Gertrude Stein in Person.* N.Y.: Rinehart, 1948.

ROSE, SIR FRANCIS: *Gertrude Stein and Painting.* 1963.

SAARINEN, ALINE B.: *The Proud Possessors.* N.Y.: Vintage Books, Random House, 1968.

SPRIGGE, ELIZABETH: *Gertrude Stein: Her Life and Work.* N.Y.: Harper, 1957.

SPRIGGE, SYLVIA: *Berenson: A Biography.* Boston: Houghton Mifflin, 1960.

STEIN, GERTRUDE: *Alphabets and birthdays.* Introduction by Donald Gallup. New Haven: Yale University Press, 1957.

————: *The Autobiography of Alice B. Toklas.* N.Y.: Harcourt Brace, 1933.

————: *Everybody's Autobiography.* N.Y.: Random House, 1937.

————: *Fernhurst, Q.E.D., and Other Early Writings.* N.Y.: Liveright, 1971.

————: *Four in America.* Introduction by Thornton Wilder. New Haven: Yale University Press, 1947.

————: *Geography and Plays.* Foreword by Sherwood Anderson. Boston: The Four Seas Co., 1922.

————: *Gertrude Stein on Picasso*, Edward Burns, ed. N.Y.: Liveright, 1970.

————: *Making of Americans.* N.Y.: Harcourt Brace, 1934.

————: *Paris France.* N.Y.: Liveright (paperback), 1970.

————: *Picasso.* Boston: Beacon Press (paperback), 1959.

————: *Selected Writings of Gertrude Stein,* Carl Van Vechten, ed. N.Y.: Random House, 1946.

————: *Things As They Are.* Vermont: Banyan Press, 1950.

————: *Three Lives.* Introduction by Carl Van Vechten. N.Y.: Modern Library, 1933.

————: *TWO: Gertrude Stein and Her Brother and Other Early Portraits.* Foreword by Janet Flanner. New Haven: Yale University Press, 1969.

————: *Wars I Have Seen.* N.Y.: Random House, 1944.

————: *The World Is Round.* Reading, Mass.: Young Scott Books, 1966; N.Y.: Avon Books (paperback), 1972.

————: *Writings and Lectures, 1909–1945,* Patricia Meyerowitz, ed. Introduction by Elizabeth Sprigge. Baltimore: Penguin Books (paperback), 1971.

STEIN, LEO: *Journey into the Self: Letters, Papers and Journals of Leo Stein,* Edmund Fuller, ed. N.Y.: Crown, 1950.

STEWART, ALLEGRA: *Gertrude Stein and the Present.* Cambridge: Harvard University Press, 1967.

SUTHERLAND, DONALD: *Gertrude Stein: A Biography of Her Work.* New Haven: Yale University Press, 1951.

TOKLAS, ALICE B.: *The Alice B. Toklas Cook Book.* N.Y.: Harper, 1954.

————: *What Is Remembered.* N.Y.: Holt, Rinehart, 1963.

VOLLARD, AMBROISE: *Recollections of a Picture Dealer.* London: Constable, 1936.

WICKES, GEORGE: *Americans in Paris.* Paris Review Editions. Garden City: Doubleday, 1969.

BIBLIOGRAPHY

INDEX